Songezwe Mahlangu

SONGEZIWE MAHLANGU

Penumbra

Kwela Books

Kwela Books,
an imprint of NB Publishers, a division of Media24 Boeke (Pty) Ltd
40 Heerengracht, Cape Town, South Africa
PO Box 6525, Roggebaai, 8012, South Africa
www.kwela.com

Cover design by publicide
Typography by Nielfa Cassiem-Carelse
Set in Zapf
Printed and bound by Interpak Books, Pietermaritzburg, South Africa

First edition, first impression 2013

ISBN: 978-0-7957-0468-0
ISBN: 978-0-7957-0469-7 (epub)
ISBN: 978-0-7957-0610-3 (mobi)

PART 1
The Moon is Dying

This is not how things are meant to be. I walk past sickly people in the street. One man's face is charred, with pink lips that have been licked by spirits. He moves like he is dying. A disabled man sits in his wheelchair in front of the Claremont BMW dealership; he looks around absent-mindedly with narrow eyes. I cross Main Road and wait for a taxi a few metres before Edgars. It does not take long for one to stop. The driver must be in his fifties. I sit in the first row facing the front. The dark-brown seats are oily and torn.

The driver is working here. The mechanics of the taxi industry mean starting the day early, transporting workers to their offices, the gaartjie opening and closing the door, collecting money, giving change and ending at home eating supper in front of the TV. We all have to work. I look out the window to my right, and see the tar sparkling in the mid-morning sun.

"The streets are empty," I say to the driver. His bald head only twitches. "Is it because of the strike?" I ask.

"The strike is starting on Thursday," a Muslim man sitting in the front says. He passes me his cellphone to show a message confirming this.

But why is he doing this? Why does he see a need to show me this message? Witches of old used to cast spells like this, by sending notes written back to front. You needed to read the note facing a mirror and would thereby curse yourself. The cellphone here is the mirror. And this man is substantiating a lie, twisting reality.

I pretend to read the message and return his cellphone. Knowing this little fact about witchcraft has saved me.

We pass a tall white block of flats, Becket's Place, in Newlands. This is where Kwanele was staying, years back, when he saw his ancestor on the back of a book in his room. At the time I dismissed it as a psychotic episode. I'm not so sure any more.

In the southern suburbs the neighbourhoods change names as you travel. Newlands becomes Rondebosch. *This is where I'm supposed to get off. But I just do not know where.* We drive past Starlite. It is empty, being a Monday morning. I ask the driver to stop opposite Pick n Pay. I stand in front of Cybar. The sky in Rondebosch is blue. Main Road groans with mid-morning traffic. The shops are stacked next to each other: Pick n Pay, Wimpy, the chemist. Thandeka, a woman who plays keyboards for a local jazz band, walks past me. She is dressed in black: black pants and a black blouse. Her eyes are yellow. I watch her approach the Van Schaik bookshop. She too is suffering. Maybe she's perishing from a lack of knowledge. She fades away from me.

I got off much later than I should have. I don't know how it escaped me that the Riverside Mall is further back. How can I forget a place I've been to so many times before? My brain shakes at this thought; wind blows in my bowels. I count my steps to the mall.

The Vertigo clothing store lies to the right of the entrance. I recognise one woman who works there. I overheard her a while back saying she had stopped drinking because alcohol made her fat. Inside, the corridors are shadowy, with a yellow cast from the lighting.

In front of a bottle store there is a blackboard with price specials written thickly in white chalk, outlined in red. The last time I bought liquor from this bottle store was during my first year at UCT. I was staying in Kopano. We had just finished writing exams.

I bought two sixpacks of Black Label cans. That time has now sadly faded.

The manufactured coolness of air conditioning blows inside the ABSA student bureau. The receptionist has long black hair, and stands behind a polished light-brown desk. I look at her for a minute. This woman is beautiful, with a glistening complexion. But there's something dark that lies in her spirit. Flies cluster in my chest. I approach her.

"Hi, I have resigned from my job. I would now like a reduced payment schedule on my student loan," I say.

"You'll have to talk to a consultant for that. She's busy at the moment," the woman says. I do not trust her. My nerves pick up speed as she talks. "You can take a seat. I'll call you when she's ready to see you."

I sit on a blue chair, take my cellphone from my pocket and check the time. It is approaching eleven. I look down at the carpet.

"You can go in," the receptionist calls out. "Go to the second door to your right."

As I walk in, the consultant is on the phone. I sit down and watch her work. She's Indian and has short hair. There is a red spot between her eyes. She puts down the phone, looks at me, inviting me to speak. I explain my resignation to her.

"Well, there's nothing we can do. You have to face the consequences of resigning without settling another job first," she splutters. While I think of what to say, she continues: "There is another option. You can contact Helen," she says, scribbling on a piece of paper.

I look at the paper and read: "Helen Messiah." The phone number contains "666".

"You can call Helen here . . ." she says, picking up the phone.

I get up and walk out.

"Where are you going?" she calls out irritably.

I do not bother to look back.

The door of a white taxi hangs open outside Pick n Pay. The gaartjie shouts: "Claremont, Wynberg." He runs after me, "Claremont, brother?" he asks. I shake my head. I walk to the shining white tiles of Pick n Pay and join the queue for airtime. A woman ahead of me takes longer than necessary. Her endless questions irk me.

In the last days, only those with the mark of the beast will be able to purchase food. My heart jumps. I get up and leave. I take deep breaths, push for calmness and stride outside to the street. *I should rather walk back to the flat. I never get it right telling taxi drivers where to drop me off. I usually ask them to stop at Crescent Clinic, which is at least four blocks before my place.*

* * *

I see the darkness of Kenilworth. It is quiet here, among blocks of flats. The shade of the many trees lends a greyness to the pavement. At this early hour the prostitutes are already working. They peddle death in Main Road, teasing the passing traffic. There is a spirit behind these women that I have only noticed today. Closer to my building, standing against a wall, is an Indian woman dressed in orange. She has sharp pointed ears. From the very bottom of my soul do I fear her. I cannot look at her for long. *What will she say if she speaks to me? Her voice will probably throw me against the wall. Then she will laugh in a hideous squeaking way.*

It is best I don't look back. I keep walking. Stale air greets me when I enter the flat. I push open the sliding window in my room. Only two windows allow air into this flat. I also open Tongai's window. His room is much smaller than mine. Having found the apartment, I chose the bigger room. Tongai has a big sheet of white paper hanging on his wall, detailing things to do: apologise to Nhlakanipho; fast for restoration.

The music of my life plays as I sit in the lounge. I am disappearing into a precarious existence. People have said many things to me. A former flatmate of mine once said that, to him, hell would be not being able to speak to those he loved. I scroll down my phone and call Ndlela. He whispers, "I'm busy at work, I'll call you at seven."

I get up to pour myself a glass of water. I once read Alice Walker who said that dying is like being pressed to pee and not being able to. I understand this. It is absorbing too much self-righteousness and not being able to release. I have been bitter for most of my life, looking for wrong in the world. In communist texts I was looking to condemn the world. I was born at five o'clock on the twenty-second of the sixth month. This season shaped my character. Perhaps it's true that people born in a certain season exhibit similar tendencies, and each season calls for its own action.

The numbers of my birth hinge on moderation. The sixth month is the middle of the year, the twenty-second day is even, and the number five is balanced – half of the perfect number ten. Perhaps this is the reason for my long-standing indecision. Even when it came to God, I doubted for a long time. *What if I have suffered the sort of death Alice Walker speaks of?* I go to the bathroom to pass water. I disappear into privacy. No one is meant to see me here. I die and come out again.

My phone beeps twice. It is a message from Paul inviting me to men's ministry at seven. I am now ready to attend. I text back to Paul: "I'm coming."

This is too presumptuous. Jesus could come before the meeting. Ndlela is also going to call me at seven. *Is there any significance to that hour? Will I be judged?* The number seven is perfect. God took seven days to create the world.

"Paul, I don't know what's wrong with me. I feel nervous. Where are you?" I say on the phone.

"I'm at work," Paul says.

"Where do you work?" I ask, hoping to go to his workplace.

"I work from home."

"Can you please come to my place?"

"Well, I have a job. I can't come right now."

"Please, Paul, do come."

"No, you want me to do what you want. I'll see you at seven," Paul says with finality.

The ANC wants a media tribunal. Maybe they are right. Behind the self-regulation of the media are people with agendas of their own. But I do not buy into this willing-buyer willing-seller slogan. The ANC has its own agenda, that of power trying to be God. People want to be God these days.

I am heating up, my head is dizzy. I walk out of the clutter of the flat into the corridor. On the ground floor a man sweeps leaves into a black refuse bag. I need someone to talk to. I hurry down the black steps to the man. He is wearing blue overalls and a green skullcap.

"Have you heard about the strike?" I ask.

"Yes, they are going to bring the country to a standstill. These strikers are going to stop everything," he says, looking at the black bag.

"No, they cannot do that. Only God has that much power," I say, running out of breath.

"They can if everyone strikes – the teachers, the nurses, the police, everyone."

This worries me. This man speaks with so much certainty. The children need to go to school. People need doctors.

"Where are you from?" I ask.

"I stay in Khayelitsha; originally I'm from the Transkei."

He says his name is Siviwe. It's an ancestral name meaning "we have been heard".

"I stay here on the first floor," I say.

"Do you live on your own? All the flats here are bachelors, right?"

"No, ours is a two-bedroom flat. I stay with a friend. He's at work right now."

"Oh, as far as I know all the flats are bachelors. This is a very old building," Siviwe says.

*　*　*

I rummage through Tongai's room. There are clothes in his wardrobe. I could not have imagined him staying with me. There are indications of Tongai: a basket with laundry in the corner, books and pieces of paper lying on the floor. Siviwe must be mistaken. Tongai has a South African ID though he's Zimbabwean. His is different from mine. The back cover of mine is at the front of his. It says he was born on the first of October. In *A Beautiful Mind*, John Nash only realised much later that his best friend was not real. "You never grow," he said.

I do not want the TV on. I sit in silence in the lounge. I do not know the name of the church I went to yesterday. It is a Portuguese church, that's all I'm certain of. When I told my mother last night that I have finally accepted Jesus Christ, she asked which church I went to. I said I did not know. This cast doubt on me. That I went into the church and didn't ask the name.

* * *

A purple cloth wipes the kitchen window. It is Siviwe. *We should be humble when people are clearing our perception.* I get up and go to him.

"You see, this is a two-bedroom flat," I say, holding the front door open.

"My friend stays in that room." I point at Tongai's room.

Siviwe enters and peers inside the flat.

"No, that room must have been constructed," Siviwe says.

Now he is the serpent. Though I have shown him the room he still has something to say. Siviwe is short. His small face grimaces as he speaks. He has come to deceive. I leave him and return to my room. Through chicanery each one of us can become the serpent. This revelation comes to me while lying in bed. I sense a snake's tongue licking. I want to spit. My spittle would be that of a cobra – venomous. The first step to deception is lying; once you lie you become like the snake. I do not ever want to mislead people. Those blessed with the word can easily galvanise people, invigorate them with rhetoric. They become the snake when doing this. From the water in my eyes, I feel the snake. Maybe it's under my bed.

I receive a call from my mother. I step out of the bedroom and into the lounge while speaking to her. She says they are happy I have accepted Jesus.

"You seemed worried last night," Mother says.

"You didn't seem happy when I told you the news, asking me which church I had gone to."

"No, we were tired. For the past weekend at church we had restoration. We were sleeping very late. How are you now?" she asks.

"I'm not well. I have this intense anxiety."

She gives me some Scripture references. I write these on a piece of paper. They are all from Psalms. I read them sitting at a table in the lounge. I plunge from one verse to the next. When the circle is complete I start again. The Scriptures catch each other. I go around, again and again. The fear does not leave me. My throat is dry from the nerves.

*   *   *

Elio can tell me the name of the church in Parow. He took me there. Over the phone we agree to meet in Mowbray. *After meeting with Elio I might as well go to Paul's place for men's ministry.* I take my Bible along for clarity. The spectacle of walking in the streets carrying a Bible does not bother me. I leave the flat wearing a grey jersey and black denim jeans. I'm back walking the same route I did earlier in the day. *They want to stop the world with this strike. Halting everything even for a minute will bring forth judgement. We believers have a lot to pray for. I really have to meet with Paul.*

I could fit into my suitcase, a body bag of sorts. In Claremont I flee past the green of the bottle store. Shops and concrete walls hang along the sides of the road. Claremont is its usual dry self, with Cavendish Square looming nearby. Chumani approaches me, carrying yellow plastic bags from Shoprite.

"It's high time you prosper, gentleman," I say, as his name translates to "prosperity".

"Are you OK?" he asks.

"I'm fine, just in a hurry to get somewhere," I say and leave him standing.

Elio and I meet at the Mowbray taxi rank, as we did yesterday. We stand in the narrow streets of Mowbray, the towering walls of Liesbeeck Gardens residence visible a little way down the road. Elio is wearing a black suit that has lost its colour. His head is small but somehow long. When I ask Elio the name of the church, he hesitates, then says it is Baptista. He says he is going to church now.

"To do what?" I ask.

"To take the pastor's place," Elio says.

This grieves me. I put out my right hand towards his chest: "In the name of Jesus," I say, my breath escaping me, and walk away.

*   *   *

I have to take a taxi to town to get to Century City. Paul stays in Century City with his wife and daughter. As the taxi fills up, I fear I will suffocate. *They are going to fill up the taxi with people till I can't breathe. This is how I am going to die.* I try opening a window. This might help, as I could jump out if need be. But I cannot move the window. I implore the driver to stop in Observatory. This is where I died, Observatory, a long time ago. My life is now being played back to me.

This is where I lost my virginity. She blew me a kiss that morning from a taxi, her caramel skin all wrinkly. I stood on the side of the road wearing my long, red Adidas T-shirt. She wore a black dress and fishnet stockings that night. We had gone to Cubaña in Newlands. I bought her drinks and watched her dance. She'd make her way towards me and grind against my loins with a naughty smile. She soon agreed to leave with me. I didn't bother informing Nhlakanipho and Mpumelelo. When we slept together I became one with her and all the men she'd known.

18

We took a cab to my residence in Observatory. But she did not want to have sex. I had to coax her. When I did pound her, I realised afterwards that the condom had split. I had semen on my pubic hair. She screamed, "See what you have done!" and went to the bathroom. I heard the sound of water falling on the tiles as I lay in bed. In the morning we went to a doctor's surgery in the backstreets of Mowbray. The doctor gave Sofia the morning-after pill and gave both of us prescriptions for anti-retroviral drugs. I stopped at Nhlakanipho's place in Newlands and asked him to go with me to a pharmacy. I poured out all my pocket money on the ARVs. We visited Kwanele in Valkenberg the same day. *God saves us so many times without us realising it. I'm sure there are people who had AIDS and whose blood he healed. Between the time of infection and getting tested a miracle could happen.*

*   *   *

I wince when I pass streetlights with "Safe Abortion" posters on them. From Observatory I cross into Salt River. I am like the wind, blowing without ceasing. I blow past the dark-brown walls of Bush Radio, leave the Caltex garage behind me. Salt River has a blueness about it from all the dilapidated buildings. At the end of Woodstock, Main Road becomes dark as I reach town. I march to the taxi rank on the station deck. It's about four and the place is teeming with people. There are boards above the bays indicating the destinations of the taxis. I can't find one pointing to Century City. I ask around and they tell me to join the queue to Milnerton. The line is long. While standing, the name "Century" plays in my mind. It is a complete number. *Am I looking for perfection?* I look in my tattered black wallet. I have one hundred rand. There is symbolism in this. A fire burns in my mind as if I'm high on weed.

I leave the line. I walk alone through the busy taxi rank. What if I cannot touch any of these people? I see a middle-aged woman with extensions in her hair. I offer her twenty rand. To be part of life I have to give to people.

"Why do you want to give it to me?" she asks.

"I just want to," I reply.

She refuses. I leave her, feeling like a madman. I really want to go to the fellowship, so I call Paul.

"How do I get to your place using public transport?"

"I don't know. Let me give the phone to my wife," Paul says.

"Hey, Manga. Look, there's a station that's just been built at Century City. You can catch a train," Paul's wife says. I walk down to the station concourse and buy a first-class ticket to Century City. I flash my ticket to a lady guard at the barrier. She lifts the steel bar, allowing me to go through. It is like an auction inside the station as a million announcements rush to my ears. I exit the station.

* * *

Back at the taxi rank, I see a guy I used to work with. I introduce myself to him.

"I know you, mfethu," he says.

"But you don't know my name," I reply. "What's your name?"

"I'm Ntobeko," he says. *This is a message. His name translates to "humility". The message is for me to be humble.*

"Were you at work?" he asks.

"No, I resigned."

"Why, what happened?"

"Some things happened . . . I fell ill."

They are all going to talk about this at the office. I was seen crazy in town. I quit my job and lost my mind. I can end up like the vaga-

bond sleeping on the stairs. My story of Cape Town: how the city beat me.

The wind pushes against my face. I amble along the blue-tar road. I call Paul again.

"I can't get to Century City," I say.

"Have you tried catching a train?" Paul asks.

"I can't. I get lost."

"I'm still busy now. Lemme pick you up later from your place," he says.

"It's fine, I believe in God," I say and drop the call. I pray for calmness. I end by saying "amen". This feels so empty, evoking the uselessness of a man's life, how it ends and how life continues. I think of Che Guevara saying "You are only killing a man." A man is something that is destined to die. The elements of life are the sun, earth, fire and water. Black people are like the sun, shining and beautiful. Somewhere we must have done wrong. We have been humbled to servants. We must take this with grace and not be bitter. Perhaps, seasons later, our beauty will return.

Paul calls back: "What's going on with you? You just hung up. Have you taken drugs? I told you I'm going to pick you up and you say you believe in God."

"No, I haven't taken drugs."

"Where are you right now?" Paul asks.

"I'm in Woodstock."

"Just find any McDonald's or KFC and wait for me there."

I go into a Debonairs and sit down. A staff member stands in front of me, wearing a black shirt. I call Paul and tell him I am at Debonairs. "OK, wait for me," he says. The assistant is speaking but I cannot make out what he is saying. He seems menacing, with a charred complexion, and speaks an exotic tongue. I force myself to calm down and stay in my seat. I have to wait for Paul. I need his help. But the fear climbs up the walls and pushes on my chest. I can't stay. I get out. I start drowning in the street. The street names keep changing. I see streets named after writers like Dickens. *Is this the passage of a writer? In the afterlife will I be assembled with writers?*

* * *

I receive a call from my mother: "I have just spoken to Bhuti Paul. He says you keep getting lost. He can't get a hold of you. Where are you?"

I look at the streets in my vicinity. I am at the corner of Dickens and Victoria roads. I'm scared of telling my mother this. It sounds like the corner of Devil and Victory.

"What I love about you, my child, is that you speak the truth," my mother says. "I have just spoken to Ndlela's father. Have you taken drugs before?" she asks.

"Yes."

"Which ones?"

"Dagga and cocaine."

My mother sighs: "Take a cab home, my child."

Ndlela's father allowed me to join Ndlela at the initiation school. I was doing my first year then. When we were preparing to return home, having been made men, a relative of mine poured oil over my head in a river, anointing me. Ndlela is one of my dearest friends. Though he works in Joburg, we still keep in contact.

* * *

I read the Bible for equanimity. It isn't consistent. The verses become different when I read over them. Evening comes. Main Road is boisterous with traffic in motion. *What did I do? I regret standing up. Things were fine when I was drinking and smoking. Maybe I need to get a drink? No, I won't.*

*   *   *

I walk in the threatening darkness, imagining myself stranded in the night, lying in some corner. This night is going to have me all to itself. My legs continue kicking through my jeans. The insides of my thighs are numb. I am desperate for people, anyone to talk to. I call Tongai; he says he is with Caroline at Trenchtown. Caroline is a Canadian who was with us the previous Saturday at a braai in Observatory. OK, I'm coming, I say to Tongai. But Observatory, as I remember when I approach the suburb, is the place of my death. I'm not certain I'll make it through or whether I'll decompose there. If I meet them they'll shake my hand like people do at the end of a race. Trenchtown is in Station Road. What will I say to Tongai and Caroline in this state? I decide not to join them.

No man knoweth the time nor the day. We do not know what will happen next. We do not even know the season we are in. Rasun, a friend of mine, had the habit of flipping a five-rand coin to decide where we should go out. He was close to the truth, for life is that precarious. I sent him an SMS on Sunday, on my way back from church with Elio, saying that God is great. Rasun responded: "Dunsky, come back to me when you've found the secret number." I deleted the message immediately. All numbers say something. One represents beginnings, two stretches to infinity; the same holds with the other even numbers. The only stable number is 666. I cannot hold on to this thought.

I cross the bridge over the N2 in Mowbray, and the wind makes my eyes water. There's an electrical substation with a grey stoep just before Forest Hill residence. Two old homeless white men used to sit on the stoep. During the day, the more vigorous one could be seen moving between the cars stopped at the traffic lights, imploring the drivers for a few cents. I stayed at Forest Hill when I was doing my postgraduate diploma in accounting. This is where I spent most of my time with Kwanele. As students we drank together and shared plenty of cigarettes. He opened me up to communism. We were bitter, looking for wrong in the world. We were insulting God with all our grief.

My head busy, I wander along the road. Around UCT the blue shuttle buses transport students to and from their residences. All I can do is walk. I'm in a dream state, eaten up with anxiety. I cannot make sense of it. I am running, rushing somewhere. The worst form of dying is to drown. You go through all the emotions, and think you are going to survive, only to die. My feet pedal above the ground. Stopping is one sure way to madness. I do not want to think about what is happening. I have to keep moving. I glide through Rondebosch, flying in the night. Soon I am in Claremont, KFC, then the taxi rank. The last thing I ate was a piece of chicken this morning. My chest is burning and my throat is as dry as the pavement. I buy a bag of apples and some juice from the ladies at the taxi rank. I eat a green apple. My chest heats up severely, and I water it down with juice. When thinking, hot coals rise to my throat and my thoughts ask each other questions, answer each other, and the answers then break into further possibilities. There is no numbness in my mind.

Carrying my Bible in my left hand, and the apples and juice in my right, I continue my journey. I am nearing home. The streetlights colour the road yellow. A homeless kid shows me his brown palms, asking for money. He stands outside the BP garage in Kenilworth. Without thinking, I give him all the coins from my pocket. "God bless," he says. This is calming and reassuring. *Where did this come from? Could he be an angel? It's probably because of the Bible. The kid is just hustling.*

A patient at the Crescent Clinic points at me. I see him in a window facing Main Road. I feel condemned. He is blaming me for something.

Seeing our block of flats makes me hopeful. I can exhale. *I am going to make it through this.* The front door is grey with rusty brown spots. I sit on the couch in the flat and catch my breath. The covering of the couch is torn, showing the yellow of the foam cushions. I put my Bible on the table. Tongai's Bible is also here; his is titled *Bible for Life Application*. These two Bibles summarise my life, with Tongai's being the book of life. *I sure am not going to find my name here.* I flip through my Bible, try reading some verses. When I reach Revelations I think I will not be able to go back. *Why are there some parts highlighted in red? This could symbolise blood.*

I did not think judgement would be like this. This is passive, filled with suggestions, yet with an air of finality.

* * *

I once held Mfundo's gun. My fingerprints are still on the weapon. I could be called in for questioning should Mfundo be arrested. With my claustrophobia I do not want to go to jail. Mfundo came in while I was sleeping on a sofa in his flat. I looked up. He was pointing the gun at me. "Mfundo, don't scare us," I said calmly, looking at him.

"No, no, no, there are no bullets. Look," he said, taking out the magazine. He then threw the gun at me. "Put it under the sofa," Mfundo said.

Maybe Mfundo shot me that night. This is all a path to my place of rest. I am being shown my life and the things that happened to me. There was also the night I broke the window in my room. I felt trapped. I tried opening the door, but couldn't. I was woken by Tongai mumbling that I would not be able to go anywhere. Next, I was pushing on the window. Tongai later told me that I suffer from night terrors. Perhaps I threw Tongai out of the window that night. And the guilt made me shut the truth away. Tongai is dead; I killed him a long time ago. Such a decent guy, who never wanted to harm anyone; I murdered him. It is this sin that is eating me up.

* * *

There are three strong knocks on the front door. I disentangle the chain.

"The people downstairs, guy . . ." Tongai says, hurrying inside with his right hand pressed against his left. He is wearing a long shirt and green cargo pants. "They say you are making a noise."

Have I been talking to myself? That could be. I pour myself a glass of water. The flat is becoming smaller. The white burglar bars could keep me captive. With my heart jerking, I go out into the corridor. Our flat is on the first floor.

"Let's go downstairs, guy," Tongai suggests.

"The body corporate say they are going to call the police."

From downstairs, a woman with dyed black hair brandishes a cellphone.

All this talk of going downstairs sounds like hell. *Is this how life draws to an end? Your friends, those who know you, usher you to hell? Going downstairs means humbling yourself, lowering your-*

self to the level of the common people. That's what these guys are trying to tell me: I haven't been humble. I even told Nhlakanipho to keep his distance from me. I judged him. I was harsh on people.

Mpumelelo approaches me, reeking of alcohol. He is wearing that grey coat of his. "You guys have been drinking . . ." I say.

"I've been drinking," Mpumelelo says, with his right hand on his chest. Nhlakanipho looks straight ahead.

"God is God. Faith is a gift. You take that first step of faith yourself," I preach breathlessly, to a cold stare from Mpumelelo.

"The Book of Job!" I shout, turning the pages of my Bible.

"Now you are talking!" Mpumelelo shouts.

I remember a poetry reading I attended with Nhlakanipho and Mpumelelo. One woman climbed on stage and said, "The Book of Job." The poem was about someone who hated his job. Perhaps the cause of my strife was quitting my job, and I just did not realise that it affected me.

I'm terrified looking at Mpumelelo. I'm stuck in the corridor. Satan awaits me downstairs. Hell is at the bottom. The guys want to hold my hands in this gnashing eternity. Mpumelelo walks away, down the stairs. For a while I'm on my own. I continue reading my Bible, my heart hammering in my chest and my head throbbing. Nhlakanipho comes towards me and opens his jacket. His cheeks are burning; he bites his mouth. I lean back and pray for strength as he gets closer.

"In the name of Jesus," I shout and release my hand with my eyes closed. I hit Nhlakanipho full in the chest. I open my eyes to see him lying on the floor.

*　　*　　*

There are cold lapses in time in which I presume Tongai, Mpumelelo and Nhlakanipho gather to strategise. I stand against the cream wall in the corridor. The sharp points in the stippled wall prick my back. I see Nhlakanipho and Mpumelelo coming towards me.

"Look at yourselves. You guys are brothers. This is all because of Nthabiseng. And she was pregnant," I pant, as the words pour from my mouth.

Mpumelelo mumbles, "We are going to beat you now." But Nhlakanipho shakes his head, scolding his older brother. I look straight at Mpumelelo.

"We are going to call the police," Mpumelelo warns.

Again, the lady from downstairs waves her cellphone.

"Call the cops. I do not fear man, I fear God," I say, absolutely hopeless.

*   *   *

They leave me in the cold with my brain frying. One tenant tries talking to me. He is wearing pyjamas. He looks like a dead man. He wants to invite me to the land of the dead. I ignore his utterances and walk to the far end of the corridor. Nhlakanipho comes back with more resolve. He harbours an unclean spirit. I have to pray for him and rid him of the demon.

"Come here," I beckon to Nhlakanipho. He stops. "Come here," I say to him again. I walk towards him, but Nhlakanipho turns around and sprints down the stairs. I run after him, but I cannot catch up with him.

Time stands still. Blood rushes to my head. Kwanele said this happened to him when he was hospitalised. There's no point in me worrying about it now.

Tongai points at Caroline. "Look, Caroline is here," he says. She looks devilish in a scarlet skirt. I have nothing to say to her.

"When is your birthday?" I ask Tongai.

He takes a sharp breath. "On the first of October," he says. Tongai once forgot his PIN number, which was his date of birth. He told me his biggest fear was getting Alzheimer's. A relative of his suffered from the disease.

"Where do you go to church?" I ask him.

"At Church on Main. You can come with me whenever you want," Tongai says, with his right hand stretched out.

"And the night terrors, how did you know about them?" I continue interrogating him.

"I told you, a lady I stayed with also suffered from them."

Sydney, with his dark locks and penetrating eyes, walks up.

"You are my brother" is what comes from my mouth. "I love all of you guys, musicians, all of you . . . Thandeka, Kgotso."

Sydney carries on the same struggle as Rasun; he is also mixed race. He could turn into Rasun. Perhaps he has come to deliver the secret number. I plunge towards Sydney and shove him back.

* * *

"If there's one thing you should have realised from this whole experience, it is just how much people care for you," Tongai says to me in the parking lot at Groote Schuur, his right arm around my shoulders. Nhlakanipho is smoking a cigarette. He passes it to Tongai when there's only a quarter remaining. I hate this about Nhlakanipho – the way he hogs a smoke.

"You were there for me when I needed your help . . ." Tongai continues. "Remember when I was locked in Tagore's. You came and helped me out."

This revelation pleases me. I look at them, Tongai and Nhlaka-nipho. These are my brothers.

"You know, I keep telling you I want to make films," Tongai says. "The first scene would open here," he says, pointing at the traffic passing on Main Road below the parking lot.

*   *   *

We took a cab to Groote Schuur. I could not go on fighting. I had to meet with my destiny. Somewhere far off I feel a pot brewing for my demise. It is either me or someone in my family who has to die. I am holding on to life, my heart scalded from the bewildering air. As we approach the main entrance to the hospital, I make it a point to walk behind Tongai and Nhlakanipho. I shake the security guard's hand and introduce myself. He is wearing khaki pants and a maroon jersey. "I am Selvyn Rooi," he says. He has no front teeth. This name means "red cell". Perhaps he is welcoming me to hell. Like a child, I follow my friends.

"Who do you think you are?" an old woman barks. She paces the floor, as wild as an animal, her hair short and grey. *Is this my grandmother? Maybe it's her.* Life has devoured her into this.

A nurse pricks my finger to draw some blood. Hospital staff hover around me. This is a thorough diagnosis. All these things are done to judge me. The diabetes test is to see whether I am too sweet. Too much of anything is not good. Blood pressure measures my warmth. Was I kind-hearted enough to people? All these things are to judge me.

Thoughts flow from my head, informing me of what's going on. *The water will turn to blood.* The water is in the drips. I am drying up. I ask for a glass of water. Drinking does not quench my thirst.

My friends are my witnesses; they attest to my character. And the doctor scribbles in his folder. Tonight Jesus has glasses, blue eyes and blond hair.

"What happened?" the doctor asks me.

"I looked into the mirror and danced . . ." I reply.

Nhlakanipho and Tongai look down.

"I realised that the world is selling us idolatry. I got tired of all these images: the TV, newspapers, magazines, internet blogs. I got tired of everything. The last time I felt like this was in high school after I smoked weed with a friend."

"Do you smoke dagga?"

"I had my first joint when I was doing grade nine. I smoked with a friend of mine, Ringo. He is dead now. He was stabbed with a screwdriver. I mostly smoked on weekends. I never abused it – not one to smoke every day. People just assumed I smoked more than I did. I only started taking drugs this year."

"Which drugs were you taking?"

"I snorted cocaine for the first time when I started hanging with Mfundo. It also became cool: the self-destruction. I wanted people to know I was on coke. One evening, on the day I had been paid, I spent almost two thousand rand on alcohol and cocaine. Later that night I scored myself a prostitute. I bumped into that prostitute not long ago. I told her that I felt very bad for having had sex with her. She looked sorry. I became too full of myself. I could even make prostitutes feel bad. Tongai came in the room when I was with the lady. He knew that I had company. He told me that he took a good look at her. What sort of a person does things like that? Since that night, I haven't taken drugs, haven't had alcohol or smoked. I broke a window in my room the week following my encounter with the prostitute. I think it was caused by stress. I felt trapped. The last time I smoked weed was when you, Nhlakanipho, came running into my flat with Mpumelelo. You were running from Mfundo. Since that day I felt nervous in the flat. I feared I'd walk in to find a gunman."

"How much does cocaine cost?" the doctor asks.

"It goes for four hundred rand," I reply.

"Four hundred rand a line?" he asks, looking shocked.

"No, they sell it in grams. It is four hundred rand a gram," I correct him.

"How much did you get paid?"

"About nine thousand rand a month. When I was young, I cursed God. I remember I was sitting on the lawn of our house in Alice. I cursed in isiXhosa."

Nhlakanipho rolls his eyes upon hearing this.

"My grandmother once came and cut all my hair with a pair of scissors. I used to have bad dreams when I was young: running in town seeing people dressed in black with necklaces of horns. Before sleeping, my grandmother used to rub me with pig fat to ward off evil spirits. I once dreamt of white women with black hair masturbating; they also had small penises."

My speech is rapid. I am not thinking. My words cut Tongai's and Nhlakanipho's eyes.

"My father I saw only once dressed in his Zulu outfit. I did not really see him. I only saw a photo. It was in his parents' home in Soweto. One morning he kept on beating me for spilling food while I was eating. His mother shouted at him to stop. I did not want to cry, but tears streamed down my cheeks. Tongai is the only person I've told that the last time I saw my father, he wanted us to take a blood test. I was fourteen years old then. I refused to go for the test. He once took me to a graveyard in Zola and spoke to the ancestors. When I hear that song by Zola, 'Bhambata', I go crazy. 'Tsotsi usus'eka Bhambata namhlanje, sofa sibalandele ba-ningi la siyakhona,'" I sing.

Tongai looks fearful as he exhales through his mouth.

"What does that mean?" the doctor asks.

"We'll die and follow them; there's plenty where we are going," I reply.

When the doctor is finished writing, he will give the verdict: whether I will make it to heaven or not. Blemishes in my spirit keep surfacing; I confess these to the doctor. In all fairness, the process is just: first the body test, the perspective from my friends, and then the verdict.

"When I was about ten years old, me and my friends called this one girl into the back room in my house. We took turns sleeping with her. I was young and I did her on top of her panties. I met her later in life; she looked like a prostitute. She died from AIDS. Guys always blamed me for Bulumko smoking weed because he first smoked with me. But then they started smoking every day. Every day after school they'd go to the park. He got expelled. I don't think he even passed matric. Whenever I met him, he was unkempt."

One at a time, Tongai and Nhlakanipho go outside with the doctor. I sit quietly with the female nurse and one of my friends. I still have my Bible in my hands. What worries me is that I'm the only one with a Bible here. Don't they realise that they need the holy book for reference? Before the doctor decides whether I'm going to heaven or hell, I have to get it all off my chest.

The doctor returns, followed by my friends.

"I went to a Portuguese church on Sunday," I tell the doctor. "It was such a surreal experience. It was like the service was custom-made for me. The preacher spoke of the issues I've had for a long time of doubting God. He said we should yield to the music of the creator. I went to meet the pastor in his office after the service. Holding his Bible, he asked me my name. It felt like he was reading from the book of life. At the flat later in the evening we were watching South African crime stories. I was scared watching the programme."

"Yeah, what was going on?" Tongai interjects.

"I thought that guy who had raped was going to turn into me. In the end I feared his face would transform into mine. I was also concerned that you, Tongai, were going to die. While in bed I had flashes of my life. Throughout my life it seemed everything had been a battle between good and evil. Is that what happens before you die, your life flashes back?" I ask the doctor.

The doctor shrugs.

I remember how I mistreated Nhlakanipho, how arrogant I was. At least Tongai was humble enough to apologise. I was walking with Nhlakanipho at about five in the morning. I was angry with him. I told him not to walk with me, to go home. I felt he was not fit to walk with me . . . That was my problem. I judged people too harshly.

"You, you speak ill of people." I confront Nhlakanipho.

He scratches his head.

"Why are you looking down? That's what you do. You never have anything positive to say about anyone. You gossip about everyone – even your own brother, Mpumelelo. That day when you were at my flat and you left thinking I was not in a good mood, what really happened was that I realised that your heart was steaming with hatred. I dreamt we were fighting that night, I was pushing you in the corridor, yelling 'In the name of Jesus'. But I did not even believe in God at the time."

Nhlakanipho only scratches his head again in reply. I address the doctor: "There's so much about Nhlakanipho that tires me. This desire of his to be the king of the castle, whatever is on offer on the table, whether it's food or liquor or cigarettes or attention, he wants the biggest chunk of it. Who gets drunk and wants to be the centre of attention? Spending time with Nhlakanipho became dreadful. He'd dump on me . . . all the problems he had with people. By the time he was done, I'd feel drained. I realised that I didn't need this in my life. I did not have to go through it; it's not like he was someone I worked with, whom I'd have to interact with."

The doctor nods in agreement.

"I did not show up for my last day of work. That was very rude of me. My contract was due to expire at the end of the year. I did not want to go back to Trilce Health anyway, so I resigned. I felt wasted there. Every day was like detention, just waiting for the day to come to an end. It's funny, afterwards, even though I was not working, I felt my time was better spent. I could do the things that I really wanted. I started writing a story. Nothing gives me greater pleasure than writing. I deleted the story five chapters in. I allowed Tongai to read it once and immediately regretted it."

"But I told you it was good," Tongai says in a gentle tone.

"Why did you regret showing it to Tongai?" the doctor asks.

"He was not being sincere. He reacted like we were at a hip-hop gig, shouting 'Blaka blaka'. I had decided a long time ago not to share my work with Tongai and Nhlakanipho. With young people there's a lot of competition. It's hard getting an honest response from them. Guys easily feel threatened."

The doctor's hand does not stop moving; he writes down everything I say. The nurse looks at me with sadness. In the hospital we passed what looked like a waiting room. The people there looked like they were in mourning.

"What was this story about?" Nhlakanipho asks.

"The theme was success. I looked at the world around me and how people measured success. To me it felt empty, the dry notion of getting a job and almost worshipping money. I was also fascinated by Mfundo: how someone could make a living out of crime; once money was in his hand it did not matter how it got there. But I deleted all of it. I thought, who am I to be telling people how to live their lives? Maybe I was trying to make a name for myself."

Nhlakanipho nods slowly.

"I hate this about Nhlakanipho, the condescension. Look at how he nodded when I said maybe I was trying to make a name for myself. He has a sharp nose for other people's weaknesses. Nhlakanipho once told me that the real poets do not get published, that the ones who perform have been told that they are good."

I am running out of breath. My heart is beating fast. I think that tonight I have to die. But life is precious, I have to fight. I used to think very little of people who feared death. But life has to be cherished. I cannot give up.

"That lady you invited to the flat was a sangoma," I say to Tongai.

"Normal life coach . . . normal life coach," Tongai grunts with a slight grin on his face and with his right hand laid over his left.

"Barefoot with dreads," I remark. "From the very first time Tongai asked me not to be around the flat, I became suspicious. I had this feeling that he was going to invite a faith healer who would sprinkle water all round the flat."

"Do you think you have any special powers?" the doctor asks me.

"No, no, I refuse that. God is God," I reply in consternation.

"One Saturday Tongai walked into the flat with a whole fried chicken," I continue. "He offered me some but I refused. I feared that the fat would clog my creativity. He seemed disappointed and said, 'Why don't you want my chicken?' I did not want to seem disrespectful so I cut two pieces for myself. When I was done eating I asked if he wasn't going to eat. He said he was not hungry. The following day the chicken was not in the house any more. I started seeing strange things at Tagore's . . . That's when this started, when I ate the chicken . . ."

No one else speaks. Tongai does not say a word. There isn't anything else that I can say.

The nurse says: "No, another one."

It seems I am preventing the doctor from attending to other patients. The doctor also seems restless. He wants me to make up my mind. If I sleep here, I do not believe I will wake up. The hospital air is freezing.

After a few moments of reflection, the doctor says: "I strongly suggest that he stays over."

I fear being hospitalised. *This will surely lead to Valkenberg. But I certainly need help.* I cannot sleep on my own at the flat. I grope for my Bible, read the verses I turn to. The others all stare at me coldly. The doctor grows impatient. "Look, you have to decide," he says. I understand, he is needed elsewhere. The nurse sighs; another patient has been admitted. I close my eyes, say a quiet prayer: "Lord, I cannot go on fighting."

* * *

In the morning I lift up my head from a white pillow. My nose is dry from the morning draught. My arms dangle in blue hospital robes. I am alive. A drip is connected through my hand. *I should quickly get out of here.* I rip off the drip with my teeth. As my feet touch the cold floor, five security guards surround me. I try pushing them off. But there's no point in fighting them. I can't. They lift me onto the bed. I watch them bind my arms in a straitjacket and attach me to the steel of the bed.

*   *   *

I scream when I wake up. A security guard runs towards me.

"What's the problem?"

"Could you please untie me? I want to go to the toilet."

"What do you want to do?"

"Number two."

He just stands there. I wet my robe, and leave a salty smell.

*   *   *

"Ahhhhhh!!!" I yell when I wake up. The same security guard comes to me again.

"What's the matter?"

"I need to use the toilet."

He just keeps quiet. I wet myself again.

Moments later, I wake to them untying me. I try not to get too excited. My mother is standing beside me. "He is going to be fine now . . ." the matron says, injecting something into my arm. Drops of water dribble off the tip of the needle. I do not feel anything.

I move my left arm around. The straitjacket has left a sweaty, swollen mark. I walk around the floor to make sense of everything. When I see the doctor who attended to me the previous night, I ask him, "How's my case looking?"

"You spent all your money on drugs and you lost your job. That's what precipitated this condition. If you take drugs again, you will end up on the streets," he says.

I smile and nod. It is chilly in here. I do not have anything on my feet. I walk back to my bed.

"Your nails are too long," my mother says. "Do you mind if I cut them?"

"No, you can."

My mother clips my toenails as I lie on my side.

"Mr Zolo, please follow me," a security guard interrupts.

The security guard takes me past a white security door to the psychiatric ward. One patient has his arms stretched out, spinning around.

"You are going to meet people worse than you. Please try not to panic," my mother whispers. She is prohibited from going beyond this point. The patient is directed to his cell by a male nurse. There is a TV playing and the patients sit around it.

I sit alone on a plastic chair. The psychiatrist is attending to a man, probably in his thirties.

"We are going to have to take you to Valkenberg," the psychiatrist says. The man breaks into tears, rubs his eyes, looking down. "We are doing this to help you."

The psychiatrist is wearing a cream sleeveless jersey and brown chinos. He is affable when he interviews me. I answer all his questions satisfactorily. I notice when he tries to trick me.

"You are from East London, right?"

"No, I'm from King William's Town," I tell him.

"What's the one thing you want to do more than anything else?"

39

"I want to write."

"Oh, a writer . . . an artist . . ." he mutters. "Is there anything else you haven't told me?"

"Like what?"

"Have you taken drugs?"

"Yes." I was afraid of saying I had taken drugs.

"Like tik?"

"No, I only took cocaine and weed."

"OK, it seems like you are fine. We are going to discharge you. You don't need any medication."

He pauses and looks at me intently.

"You must write, whether you get published or not," he advises me.

I nod.

My mother hugs me when I tell her I have been discharged.

My Bible is in a clear plastic bag, like a piece of evidence. I get it from one of the nurses.

"You really looked like you were going to die last night," one nurse says.

* * *

I sit on the bed, having taken a shower and got dressed. Nhlaka-nipho calls me on my mother's phone.

"Tongai took your wallet and your cellphone for safekeeping," he says. "How are you feeling now?"

"I'm much better," I reply.

"I can tell you're fine now," Nhlakanipho says.

"It was a spiritual battle," I say.

"We'll talk later," he says, ending the call.

Heavy rain shoots down in the bitter wind. The cold creeps

into the wooden shelter for the security guards where my mother and I wait for Tongai to bring the apartment keys. He gets out of a colleague's car and runs up to us. He has a blue cap on his head.

He smiles and presses his right hand against his left when he greets my mother.

Tongai runs back to the car. He and his colleague are off on some work trip. My mother and I walk down the hill from Groote Schuur. At the bus stop on Main Road, we wait for a taxi. It is mid-morning. Nurses trickle up the road to the hospital. Behind us is Texie's fish and chips shop. I hold up my index finger, seeing a cream-coloured taxi approaching. The vehicle halts and the gaartjie drags the door open for us. The only available seats are at the back. I sit closest to the window to the right.

Things are hazy to me. I'm just grateful to have made it out of the hospital. My nerves have calmed. I whisper to my mother how much money she has to pay. The taxi drives down the wet road. I am looking out the window.

* * *

As the taxi approaches the first group of flats in Kenilworth, I ask the driver to stop. My mother and I walk the rest of the way to my apartment building. The woman from the body corporate hovers in the yard as I open the gate. She is wearing a long black gown.

"I do not trust her," I say to my mother.

"She seems like she could be one of these gypsies," Mother responds.

We place our bags in my bedroom. Things have never been open between my mother and me. She was only eighteen when she had me, during her first year at varsity. And so she left me with my grandmother. When she started working in Joburg, I used to visit her. For a while, she was living with my father in Joburg. We've always had a distant relationship. Even when Mother started staying with us, in my high school years, we never warmed to each other. But she supported me throughout university, paying for my fees and sending me pocket money.

In the afternoon, I decide to cook. I defrost some boerewors from the freezer. Mother sits in the lounge while I chop onions. I make rice and mixed vegetables to accompany the meat.

Mother says grace once the food is ready. We eat in the lounge. There's a copy of *Chimurenga*, with Brenda Fassie on the cover, lying on the coffee table.

"My father predicted that Brenda would be a star," Mother says, after looking through the magazine.

"What happened to your father? How did he die?" I ask.

"My father . . . he died from a heart attack."

I have never been able to ask what happened to my grandfather. We have a picture of him in our living room at home. He died a couple of years before I was born.

"I was under intense attack when I fell ill," I say.

"Those demons didn't want you to come into contact with Bhuti Paul," Mother says. "It's probably because of that church you went to. I have heard of similar things happening to people who attended Universal Church. In some cases they were not even able to make contact with their family. They would be in the same place and would not be able to see each other," she explains.

"Tongai also attends a strange church. He doesn't want any of us to ever go with him to church. He says he becomes a different person in there. Tongai also has his things. There are times that he asks me to vacate the flat when he has to meet with his life coach," I say.

Mother keeps quiet and continues eating.

"I didn't know you could cook this well," she says.

I shrug. I had to teach myself to cook when I started staying in a self-catering residence. It wasn't that hard.

"You know, what I really want to do is to write," I say suddenly.

"I didn't know that. I never would have imagined it, considering your brilliance with numbers," Mother responds.

She's right; I have always excelled in mathematics. But since high school I have had the idea that one day I would be a writer. In my last two years at university, I became increasingly isolated. Studying accounting felt meaningless. What surprises me is my mother's calmness at my revelation. For some reason, I had always assumed that she just wanted me to make money.

"Well, we'll have to figure out a way for you and your writing," she suggests.

*   *   *

We have to buy air tickets for our trip back home. We head to Rondebosch, to the travel agency in the Riverside Mall. The earliest flight we can get is on Sunday. At night, Mother sleeps in my bedroom. I take the lounge.

*   *   *

The next day, in the early evening, they all come to see me: Mpumelelo, Nhlakanipho, Tongai and Nhlakanipho's girlfriend, Lesego. It is my first time meeting Lesego. She looks dry, with thin hair. Mpumelelo appears yellowy in his grey coat. I smell brew on Mpumelelo's breath. I look him in the eyes, shake his hand; he nods, with fear all around him. I sense Nhlakanipho's heavy eyes from the side. As I approach Lesego I become aware of my baggy shorts and skater tackies. She puts out a feeble hand and nods nervously.

I offer them something to drink. Mpumelelo jumps up first. "I want some," he says with his right hand on his chest. I pour each a glass of Tropika. The gathering is awkward. No one mentions my breakdown. Nhlakanipho drove to my place. He has hired a car for the weekend. Moments later, he gets up. His belly protrudes through his golf shirt. He is wearing black sandals.

"I have to take Lesego home," he says.

I see them out of the flat. Mpumelelo stops, looking like he has forgotten something; he goes to my room and bids my mother goodbye.

*   *   *

Tongai says that I was extremely strong on the night of my breakdown. My remembrance of the events surprises him.

"That's the part I find very strange," he says.

I confide to Tongai that I thought judgement was nigh, that I feared Armageddon would take place at seven, as people wanted to meet me at that specific hour.

"I understand why Kafka wanted to have all his writing destroyed after his death," I say to Tongai.

"It was a matter of the heart. Only he knew where his heart was at the time he wrote those books. Leaving lasting works when you know your heart was not in the right place would be hell. Those who went ahead and published his writing were wrong."

"Hayi, the dead have no rights!" Tongai bursts out. Then he puts his hands together and looks contrite. I read his regret at

his brash utterance. Tongai often makes remarks and then says
he's sorry. Apologies are a part of his nature.

* * *

Tongai dashes out to work in the morning. He is an intern at an
advertising company in town, and works until noon on some
Saturdays. A while back, he had to package CDs that were to be
distributed to taverns promoting Three Ships whisky. I assisted
him that day, and it was tedious.

A faint sunlight smiles through the window in my room. I
vibe to Gil Scott-Heron, peaceful melodies transporting me to a
land of spirits. Since the beginning of this year, I have acquired
the habit of recording life in a journal. I have to write about the
madness of the past few days, but my journal is not on my desk.
I ransack my room looking for it.

"Have you seen a black notebook?" I ask my mother.

"No, I haven't."

"This is very strange, I usually keep it on my desk."

I call Tongai at his work. "Do you know where my diary is?"

He takes a few breaths before answering. "It's at my mom's
house. Me and Nhlakanipho, we were looking for clues as to what
caused your breakdown," he explains.

"No, I don't like what you did. So you read my diary?"

"No, we didn't, serious . . . we didn't."

"I don't like what you did."

"The diary is in my bag in the lounge," Tongai finally says.

I find the notebook in the bag. I no longer have the urgency to
write. I wonder what they saw in my diary. I'm even afraid of
looking at what I have written.

My mother placates me by saying that when someone has gone

through an experience such as mine it is only natural for people to look for clues. She calls Tongai to apologise on my behalf. Tongai tells her to tell me that he'll be watching rugby later in the afternoon. At about three I join Tongai at Café Sofia in Rondebosch, upstairs from the Pick n Pay. Inside there are round brown tables. The floor has brown tiles. There is a vibrant feel to the place, with young students serving as waiters. Tongai sits with intent at the table, wearing the round glasses he recently bought. His previous pair was lost during a drunken night out. Tongai has a glass of draught beer in front of him. For this game – South Africa against Australia – he supports Australia. I find this odd. Black guys usually support New Zealand when they don't favour the Springboks. I am not at all interested in the match. Even though I attended a boys' school, where rugby was a religion, I have never had a liking for the sport. To Tongai's pleasure, Australia wins the game.

Nhlakanipho and Mpumelelo had gone to Mzoli's in Gugulethu. They join us later at Café Sofia. Mpumelelo orders a beer. Nhlakanipho is still trying to stop drinking. He has orange juice.

"You know what I observed at Mzoli's?" Mpumelelo ventures. "Everything depends on money. You know, the chicks look at what the guy is drinking. Everyone goes there with a car."

Nhlakanipho shakes his head, not impressed by what his older brother is saying. He yields to his craving and calls a waitress to order a beer. I keep quiet, not paying attention to what the guys are saying. With a car for the weekend, Nhlakanipho wants to make the most of this mobility. He suggests they go somewhere else. As if he can read my mind, he offers to drop me off at home.

* * *

I lie on the couch tucked under a duvet. I have been reading *Nausea* by Jean-Paul Sartre for a while. Now, I find I cannot absorb the book. The feelings of the meaninglessness of everything seem stale. When I told Rasun I was reading *Nausea* he said he didn't like the book. He has always had more of a penchant for life.

The creak of the door wakes me. It is Nhlakanipho and Tongai. They take a seat on the other couch to my right. Nhlakanipho's eyes are bloodshot.

"You know, what we have realised from this whole experience of yours . . . is just how sadistic we can be," Nhlakanipho says coolly, caressing his belly.

I grunt at this statement. My reaction is almost reflexive. Nhlakanipho does not take this further. For several heartbeats we sit in silence.

"I even regret hiring this car now," Nhlakanipho says. "There's no way they won't notice the scratch."

"You have to explain it to them," Tongai advises.

"What were you doing with this car anyway?" I ask Nhlakanipho.

He does not reply.

"I was trying to sleep, gents," I say. Nhlakanipho mumbles good-bye to me. Tongai sees him out.

*   *   *

In the morning, while we pack, I make a point of taking all my diaries with me. Tongai accompanies us in the taxi. He is on his way to church, and is carrying his big brown Bible. He gets off in Claremont. Mother and I continue to the airport. The taxi driver drops us off in the loading zone. I push our luggage in a trolley into the terminal. The airport is not that busy. Our flight is scheduled for half past twelve. We check our luggage at the airline counter.

For breakfast, we go upstairs to the Wimpy. I have brought two books to read on the plane: *Summertime* by JM Coetzee and *The Will to Die* by Can Themba. Mother glances at the books while we sit at the Wimpy.

We eat breakfast, go downstairs and wait for our flight. I board the plane, carrying my books in my backpack. I know the Cape Town – East London route all too well. I have been flying it since my first year at varsity. The planes are very small, with only two seats in each row on either side of the narrow aisle. I feel claustrophobic as soon as we enter the plane. Seeing the door close frightens me even more, though the announcement of the exit doors calms me. It introduces an element of control. *I am not entirely trapped.*

About ten minutes into the flight, a flight attendant comes down the aisle. "Would you like anything to drink?" she asks.

"I'd like some grape juice," I reply.

She passes us our meal packs. Lunch is a cold chicken burger and a bar of chocolate. We eat as the plane buzzes through the clouds.

* * *

In East London, we wait for our luggage around the conveyor belt. I run to the front upon spotting my bag. Mother brought only one suitcase with her. Once we have placed our bags on a trolley, we make our way outside. The East London airport is much smaller than the one in Cape Town. Here there are only two levels; everything happens on the ground floor, with a few restaurants on the top floor.

The electronic doors slide open as we walk out of the terminal. There are a few cars parked close to the entrance. These are usually cars of VIPs. Mother had left her car parked at the airport while she was in Cape Town. It takes a few minutes to find the car. We pull out of the parking lot. Mother inserts the parking ticket into the machine and we drive out of the airport. Soon we join the highway leading to King William's Town. The car radio is playing "Nizalwa ngobani" by Thandiswa Mazwai. For a while, only the song matters. It gives me brief happiness.

The trip takes us about half an hour. Pink and orange RDP houses appear as we approach the signboard that welcomes us to King. We turn off the highway and pass the BP garage. Up close, the houses are dilapidated, the paint peeling. We drive into our suburb. It is a quiet neighbourhood with families of moderate means. Mother stops in front of our gate; I get out of the car to open it. It's been this way since high school: whenever we went to town, I would have to open the gate. Before we even enter the house, my grandmother comes out to meet us. She looks older than the last time I saw her. It always worries me seeing her grow old. She gives me a brief embrace. My grandmother is someone who worries a lot. She has a panicked air, and is easily startled; you can pick it up from the way she breathes. Even now I can tell that she is uneasy.

Our house has neat lawns at the front and back. The house itself is painted peachy orange. The gate is low; someone could easily jump over it. We have a black-and-white postbox above a pillar at the front gate. We know our neighbours only by name; there is no other connection. I found this quietness and coldness frustrating when we first moved to King from Alice. The streets were hauntingly still. But I got used to it over the years.

*   *   *

As soon as I have settled at home, I send Tongai a message to say we have arrived safely. His response is "Blessings, brethren", a phrase he has never used to me before. I swallow it with suspicion.

Things seem smaller at home – the TV, everything. There are five of us in the three-bedroom house: my grandmother, my mother, my aunt and her daughter and myself. We have a domestic worker, Ma'Dlomo, who comes in weekdays to clean. My grandmother cooks in the evenings. Before going to bed, we convene in the lounge. We each read a passage from the Bible and we close with a prayer. I used to try to find something vilifying in the past: I'd read a verse about the Israelites being God's people. When it was time to pray I would just kneel and close my eyes, waiting for them to finish.

My only chore is to go out and buy bread and the newspaper. On one of my trips to the store, I hear a whistle from behind. It's a friend of mine, Luvuyo, emerging from Diva's, a liquor den. He asks me to buy him a beer. I'm no longer working, I tell him. I sense his disappointment. It feels like he expected more from me.

"Come chill with us inside," Luvuyo suggests.

"There are some loose ends I have to tie up," I say.

This town carries pieces of me. We used to attend a church youth programme on Fridays when we were in high school. For Bulumko and me, it was a chance to smoke weed. We'd go there stoned. I lost a lot of weight and people kept asking me if I was well. I was finicky about eating. Before I went to sleep, I'd lie in bed thinking of all the food I'd had during the day. The less I ate, the more pleased I was. I had started gaining weight when we moved to King William's Town from Alice. By the time I was in grade seven I had become fat. That's how the silence began. Gradually I spoke less and less. I was shaken one year when my mother came down from Joburg for the holidays and didn't recognise me. I had become skeletal. From that moment, I started eating again.

My grandmother has been retired for close to ten years now. She basically raised me and is the only parent I really know. In this house she beat me disciplining me when I was naughty. When I came close to dying, I realised just how much I loved her.

A childhood friend, Siyabonga, lives in the street below ours. He was with Ringo on the night of the stabbing. For many years he has been applying for jobs. He did a couple of semesters at the University of the Free State, but left when his father lost his job and could no longer pay his fees. Together we laugh about our age-mates in government, with their inflated bellies and behinds. These working men frequent a tavern close to the train station on weekends. They carry trays laden with meat and alcohol.

The horizon is purple as we sit in front of Siyabonga's house. When he asks me why I quit my job, I tell him that I got tired of working for coloureds. That's how it is in Cape Town, I explain. Soon the sky darkens, the conversation dries up and we part ways.

* * *

We take turns in the bathroom on Sunday morning while preparing for church. The hot water runs out after the first two people have bathed. I have to heat my water on the stove. I'm very fussy about bathing. I cannot wash with cold water as it gives me a neurotic itch. We leave my aunt behind at the house and drive to Bhisho in my mother's BMW 3 series. Dishevelled young men in the parking lot outside the church busy themselves washing the cars. My mother raises her hand, signalling to the young man who usually cleans her vehicle. He runs towards us carrying a bucket and a sponge.

The church is an expansive orange building that used to be a Cash and Carry. It is right in the centre of Bhisho, past the garage and the police station. Bhisho is a little town of civil servants. There are a few shops that cater for the small populace. We worship surrounded by government offices.

My mother and grandmother walk to the chairs closer to the front. I take a less conspicuous position at the back. Our pastor is a light-skinned man in his mid-thirties. He wears a three-quarter gold suit like the ones worn by the preachers on TBN. He used to attend our fellowship in Alice when he was still a student at Fort Hare, my grandmother tells me. I must have been five years old back then. His passionate singing draws me into the worship. I join in to sing. I have never been much of a singer. I was always told that I was out of tune. The preaching loosens wires in my throat.

"You should brace yourself for stormy times when you ask God to make you right," the pastor says.

"As you come from that period your return will be multiplied tenfold. But don't expect God to reward you the way you want him to. See, God is a God of covenants; he sticks to his agreement. Samson had long fallen off. When he was with Delilah he had already backslidden. But God's word was: 'No meat and no wine.'"

The pastor looks off into the horizon.

"Do not wish to be in another person's position. You do not know that person's struggles. Why you were born, where you were born – do not question those things. See, people in the world want to have certain achievements and things at certain times in their lives. What they forget is that there are also God's seasons. There are seasons that God sets in your life. When those seasons come, you better be prepared.

"Do not curse God when he is purifying you. Accept the challenges that come your way. If this is your will, God, then let it be, you should say. Remember, God says: 'My grace is sufficient.'" The pastor lifts up his right hand and stares into the distance again.

Sweet tears stream down my cheeks. *My time is still coming; life ain't over. I might not have the accessories that some of my age-mates have, but my turn will also come.* Our pastor has been working hard for a long time. Week in, week out, he finishes the service with his jacket sticking to his sweaty back. As a university student, I doubted him when he said circumcision was demonic. In those days I was into Black Consciousness and saw him as demonising African tradition. My acceptance of Christ has required me to get out of my mind, for spirituality is not an exercise of intellect. It's like Paul says: "These battles are not of the flesh and blood."

At the end of the service the pastor calls for people interested in joining a transformation programme to be held in East London to stay behind. I have been humbled. Work is work to me, irrespective of titles or prestige. This initiative would allow me to make a contribution. I write down my details in the roster that is passed around. The only problem is that I'll be heading to Cape Town in a couple of weeks' time to clear the flat. I'll have to miss the first session.

* * *

My mother says Tongai is a very sweet boy. She prays for Tongai and Nhlakanipho, asking God to forgive their sins. She even wants to call Tongai to find out if he's well.

"Your friends were very worried about you," my mother says. "Nhlakanipho almost cried when he explained that they did not have a choice. They had to take you to hospital."

PART 2
A Turn Under the Sun

I came back to Cape Town at the beginning of the year. I was returning to a job that had no life for me. It was my second year at Trilce Health. As soon as I stepped out of the domestic terminal at the airport, I bought a packet of ten cigarettes. For the two weeks I had been at home, I had not smoked or drank. I did not want my mother and grandmother to know of my debauchery.

I was renting a room in a four-bedroom house in Observatory. It was Victorian and had a porch supported by white pillars. The house was in the part of Observatory that is very close to Salt River.

On entering, I dragged my bag along the floor to my room, the first door on the left. The room had an iron bed. One woman I slept with in that bed complained about it not being a bed but rather a plank of wood. I dreaded the first night back at the boarding house – that empty hazy feeling of stony beginnings. I kept going outside to smoke on the porch.

My housemates had just about all returned from the holidays. One guy had gone back to Joburg. We could never get along. Though he was younger than me, he was authoritarian and often complained about my untidiness. He addressed me with disdain. Once he asked the other tenants if they'd ever encountered anyone as strange as me. This hostile attitude from my housemates made me want to leave the house. I had told the landlady before the holidays that I wanted to move out. I had until the end of January to find new accommodation. *Things will hopefully be easier in an apartment that I'll share with one person.*

Once back at work, I looked on the Gumtree website for a place to stay. One available room was in Green Point. I made arrangements to view the place on a Saturday afternoon. I caught a taxi from Observatory to town on that Saturday. From the taxi rank in town, I took another taxi to Green Point. I got off on Main Road. People sat casually in front of restaurants or strolled along the street. Seen through my frameless glasses, the sun irradiated the world on that summer's day. Construction was still under way on the new stadium, which took a bite from the sky. I asked for directions from an old woman walking her dog. She pointed me to the residential side of the neighbourhood. The sunshine pierced through the houses.

Near the bottom of a steep street stood the place I had come to see. It was cream with light-brown window panes. The two-bedroom apartment was leased by a white student in his third year at UCT. He was uncomfortable as he showed me around. When I had finished viewing the flat, he took down my details, saying more people were still coming to see the room. I nodded and said I was looking forward to hearing from him. I doubted that he'd call me.

I had not solved my accommodation problem. At the station in town, unsure of whether I should go home, I decided to visit Nhlakanipho in Newlands. I had gone to high school and university with Nhlakanipho. He stayed with his brother, Mpumelelo, in a block of flats just around the corner from the train station. Nhlakanipho's street was always shadowy. I guess it had to do with the tall trees.

I found Nhlakanipho and Mpumelelo sitting with a sixpack of Castle in their dark lounge. They had an old 72 cm TV on top of a dark-brown coffee table. I helped myself to a beer and lit a cigarette. It was the dry part of the month. Mpumelelo started singing his song: "I get embarrassed when people come in here, look at how untidy this flat is, not having money sucks, look at how we live drinking the same beer, we should alternate, have cocktails on some occasions, I haven't given up on making it . . ."

Nhlakanipho echoed Mpumelelo, leavening the song with anecdotes of the embarrassment of being broke. Mpumelelo's screensaver on his computer was a Range Rover. It was the car he aspired to drive once he had made it. The brothers disregarded those who did not share their ambitions.

That was when Mfundo walked into the apartment through the open door. Nhlakanipho had told me about Mfundo. He stayed in a bachelor flat on the ground floor.

He waved his right hand and sat down. Soon he got up. "I have some beers downstairs," he mumbled on his way out.

"Don't be surprised if he comes back with coke," Nhlakanipho whispered, pulling his nose. Mfundo came back with champagne for himself and a sixpack of beer for us. The coke was in a note wrapped up like a Grand-Pa headache powder. He scooped up the white powder with a bank card, snorted up his left nostril, closed his eyes, and then sniffed up his right nostril. He passed the note to Mpumelelo. Nhlakanipho and Mpumelelo snorted. I declined.

"I told my mom a long time ago," Mfundo said, "'Those white boys you sent me to school with are now working in their uncles' companies. This is my life, drinking in my back room, money from stealing car radios.' When she asked, 'What if you get arrested?', I said I'll see that when it happens. When I got locked up, she was my first visitor in Pollsmoor." Mfundo spoke fast, sounding like he had a blocked nose.

"See, my younger brother, he works as an accountant. That

laaitie, he was so full of kak, the time he was at UCT. These degrees don't mean anything because he's now working for someone else. What really matters is being able to read people. Like, I can see Nhlakanipho, he likes nice things. You, Mangaliso" – he pointed at me – "you are quiet and observant. Mpumelelo, he talks a lot and probably also lies a lot. Everyone is doing it for themselves nowadays. That's why I feel sorry for cops who don't want to take bribes. Look at Jackie Selebi," Mfundo said, laughing.

We joined in the laughter. Mfundo controlled the conversation and we listened. Only thirty, he looked much older than his age, with a large belly disproportionate to his small legs. He had grown up in boarding schools, first in Grahamstown and later, after getting expelled, at Rondebosch Boys' High. He had a curious taste for politics, speculating on the underworld of the ruling party. Mfundo related to Nhlakanipho on this level. Since our high school days, Nhlakanipho had had a keen interest in politics. This had gone on to inform his social persona. He often called people "chief".

As night fell, Mfundo suggested we visit one of his grootmans. We took the remaining beers and champagne along. Nhlakanipho and I sat in the back seat of his BMW M3. Nhlakanipho held Mfundo's champagne, and Mfundo assigned him to refill his glass while he drove. Mpumelelo was in the passenger seat. Mfundo and Mpumelelo got along handsomely.

We filled the car with petrol at the Engen garage in Newlands. There was a white woman parked next to us; her son was helping the petrol attendant by holding the pump.

"He won't be a doctor," Mpumelelo remarked from the front seat.

The woman chuckled, acknowledging the attempt at humour. From the garage we drove down Main Road, with Mfundo gyrating to the house music he was playing. As we passed a group of bergies at the Liesbeek River, Mfundo said: "The problem with these fuckers is that they are lazy. You can try to give them something . . ." Mfundo pulled his mouth, shaking his head. "Me, I can get told to get five cars in one night and I won't ask any questions." We shot down the highway, zigzagging to the northern suburbs.

We stopped opposite the Spur in Big Bay. Night had cooled the air. A few cars passed us. The familiar image of the Indian warrior was stuck to the restaurant window. The others continued stuffing their noses with cocaine. I noticed a police car drive past us. A few minutes later the same police vehicle drove back. I pointed this out to Mfundo.

"Don't worry, that's a Bon Jovi. They understand protocol. The difficult ones are the police vans," he advised.

The car stopped next to us. A white man dressed in blue with a bulletproof vest came towards us. Mfundo folded the cocaine note and pushed it into his wallet.

"What's going on here?" the policeman asked outside Mfundo's window.

Mfundo lowered the tinted window and smiled at the officer.

"Oh, Mr Mnyamana, it's you," the policeman remarked.

Mfundo laughed, squeaking through his throat, nodding.

The officer left after an exchange of pleasantries with Mfundo.

"This one . . . he really understands protocol," Mfundo said. "I once had a case. When I walked into court, the magistrate started laughing. When they asked him why he was laughing he told them that I used to teach him maths. I got off that case scot-free. So you never know when you will need someone."

Mfundo received a call from the man we were to visit.

"We can go now," Mfundo said. "I was waiting for the call, it's protocol. Had he not phoned me it would have meant he did not want us there."

We drove through Table View. It was a quiet neighbourhood, with the houses close to one another. This was my first time in the northern suburbs. I was used to the southern suburbs.

"This is a place for the emerging blacks, the ones that are not that wealthy yet," Mfundo said.

We parked outside a double-storey facebrick house. There was a Mercedes-Benz sandwiched between two trucks in the yard.

"This is how it's done. You put working trucks in the front," Mfundo muttered.

The gentleman we had come to see, Bra Menzi, came out wearing a T-shirt and jeans. His skin was taut and his well-built upper body clearly suggested he worked out. His wife was rocking their newborn child in the kitchen. We introduced ourselves and went upstairs to Bra Menzi's bedroom. It was spacious, with a furry brown carpet. We watched football on the 102 cm plasma screen. Bra Menzi brought us a bottle of Veuve Clicquot champagne. Nhlakanipho filled his glass, showing great excitement.

"I really like your house, grootman," Nhlakanipho said.

"Thanks, mfethu," Bra Menzi replied.

We were allowed to smoke only on the balcony. We were careful not to drop ash on the floor and we kept the butts in the packet. In spite of all the cocaine the guys were taking, I did not see any change in their behaviour. When Mfundo produced another batch, I took a couple of lines. The white powder went up my nostrils, leaving my throat dry. I struggled to wet my larynx with saliva. My heart started beating faster than usual. I sat in great discomfort on the couch.

Bra Menzi stayed inside while we dabbled with drugs on the

balcony. He was most obliging. When the bottle of champagne was finished, he took out another one.

"So, gents, where do you stay?" Bra Menzi asked.

"I stay in Observatory," I said.

Nhlakanipho quickly added: "We stay upstairs from Mfundo's place."

Bra Menzi nodded.

Mfundo spent a lot of time outside with an associate discussing their affairs. He said that there was a war going on and that it would be dangerous for us to go to the location with him. We cut through the night streets back to Newlands.

*   *   *

Mfundo's girlfriend, who was visiting for the weekend with their five-year-old daughter, had prepared macaroni and mince in Mfundo's flat. We served ourselves portions. Mfundo kept what he called his magic bag – a pouch stuffed with banknotes – slung over his right shoulder. The flat was carefully decorated, with animal skins on the floor. After eating, we left the flat to go to Nhlakanipho's place. Mfundo sauntered out, his hips moving sharply from side to side. He gave us each five hundred rand from his bag to go out.

"You are now part of the family," Mfundo said in a gentle tone before going back into his apartment.

"Let's spend the dirty money!" Nhlakanipho crowed.

Nhlakanipho and Mpumelelo put on clothes for going out, both wearing blue T-shirts and sneakers. The cocaine in my system made me feel rebellious. I wanted to wear a panama to cover my eyes. Mpumelelo took it off, saying, "This thing is meant to be worn during the day."

"I can't believe I let him put it on," Nhlakanipho said, then became embarrassed when I looked at him.

I yielded to their pressure and did not wear the panama, though I was slightly irritated.

*   *   *

We walked confidently up Long Street, money in our pockets, and strolled into Marvel. The club was full, pop rap music blaring from the speakers. I struck up a conversation with two girls. We were sitting in front of the door, with a black rope forming a square around us. The girls were second-year drama students. Mpumelelo went to get drinks for everyone.

Nhlakanipho, who could be a nuisance when drunk, was laughing with some women nearby.

"What do you know about Versace?" I heard him say loudly.

When I looked up, one of the women was on her feet, telling Nhlakanipho to leave them alone. The bouncers came and escorted Nhlakanipho out. We could no longer stay at the club.

*   *   *

I sang my own composition in the shower on Sunday morning: "Sexy crime / beautiful crime / it's enough to die."

Sunday is a short day that threatens to fade in a few hours' time. My housemates bought beers from Auntie's. We sat on the porch. There was also weed. I alternated between smokes and joints. I tried telling my housemates just how seductive crime can be. But they never seemed to have the time to listen to me. As soon as I started speaking, they looked bored.

*   *   *

I trudge in to work around eight-thirty each morning with my backpack on and take the lift to the fourteenth floor. By the time I enter the office, most employees are already at their desks. I pass them nervously, greet my colleagues in my section and sit in my cubicle. I surf the internet for two hours and then it's teatime. I fill a mug with tasteless coffee from the machine and get back to the internet.

I rotated into this new department in the hope of getting more work. I spent three months in my previous function doing nothing. Those accepted into the graduate programme at Trilce are supposed to work on high-level projects and be moulded into future managers. After failing my postgraduate diploma in accounting, I did not have the energy or the will to repeat it. I never liked accounting, and only decided to major in business science after flipping through the newspaper and seeing the high salaries earned by financial managers. I bumped into the Trilce job on the internet in the season after I failed my diploma. I could no longer follow my intended path of doing my articles and becoming a chartered accountant. I did not do well on the psychometric tests, and only got into the programme when one of the other graduates pulled out.

I remember seeing my results on the noticeboard at the Leslie Commerce Building at UCT. I had failed all my courses save for ethics. I breathed in a peculiar disappointment; I was not too surprised. When I wrote about this experience in the computer lab at Forest Hill and showed the piece to Kwanele, he angrily dismissed it: "Are you going to make them read this? How can you write about yourself?" he asked. "There was one writer who had a book called something like 'why I'm the smartest man alive'," Kwanele explained. "What I'm trying to say is that you should avoid this egocentric writing. Any book of importance touches on the politics of the time. My advice to you is that if you ever want to write, you must represent people."

I left Kwanele, saying that I'd be looking for a job in the coming year. "I worry when someone says that finding employment in this country is so hard," he said. I did not continue with that piece of writing.

Other employees bring their takeaways to the office. I do not like eating inside, so I have my lunch at KFC or Nando's or at a place that sells Cape Malay fast foods. I find a discreet spot under a tree to have my cigarette, gently drawing the smoke into my lungs with the taste of food still in my mouth. When I'm finished, I suck a sweet on my way back to the office. The rest of the day passes swiftly. We are meant to work eight hours each day, excluding lunch and tea. Because I come in at eight-thirty, I'm meant to go home at half past four, but when the clock strikes four I leave the office.

* * *

I visited Nhlakanipho one Saturday evening. He asked me if I could buy some beers and bring them along. Nhlakanipho was not working at the time. He had resigned from his job the previous year. The bottle store was closed, so I came back empty-handed. Nhlakanipho and Mpumelelo were watching TV in their dim lounge. It was a sour evening; Nhlakanipho had spiteful things to say.

"Do you remember that girl you had a thing for . . . Zandi?" Nhlakanipho said.

"She used to say, 'Manga is going to be an accountant'," Nhlakanipho said, emulating Zandi and laughing coldly. I held my breath and nodded at the anecdote. I left. Nhlakanipho's prickly words had pierced me.

*   *   *

To be a competent writer I have to learn the technical aspects of the craft. I search for writing workshops on the internet at work. I find one in Rondebosch. I send an e-mail to the woman responsible, expressing my interest. She gets back to me in no time. They are starting on Thursday, she says. I must pay eight hundred rand for the four sessions.

After five on Thursday afternoon I amble up Polo Road to catch a taxi on Main Road. I get off in Rondebosch in front of Stardust. The woman's house is in Rouwkoop Road. She opens a white security door to let me in. Inside, the other learners are already seated around a white table in the study area, next to an all-white kitchen. A brown and white cat roams through the house. We each give our reasons for writing. A middle-aged white man says he is fascinated by sangomas and wants to write about them, merging Western medicine with African practices. We hear a thudding sound coming from the ceiling.

"There are so many spirits in these old houses," our instructor says. "Imagine how many people have stayed here."

An eerie sensation pricks me on my cheeks and on my back. I do not believe in God, let alone spirits. I did not know white people could be this superstitious.

"I have been inspired by people like Zakes Mda," I say, when my turn comes. "I have always wanted to write about my world and tell it the way that I see it. In the past I have written poetry and have performed in various subculture events."

"Oh, so you already know you are creative?" the instructor asks.

I nod. One book she suggests is *The Artist's Way*. She gives us an assignment for the next week, titled "The view from the window".

* * *

When I wake early enough, I catch a train to work from Salt River station. Taking a train works out much cheaper than a taxi and you don't have to put up with rude gaartjies. A dreadlocked woman is walking down the stairs in the station. Her behind rounds her faded denim jeans; her thighs do not touch. I cannot help myself. I have to talk to her. I follow her and stand next to her. Her name is Noziqhamo; she is from Langa. She works for a catering company. She has narrow eyes and her skin is tight on her face. She says she doesn't give her number to strangers. You can break that rule, just this once, I plead. She gives in to my persistence. I save her number on my cellphone.

* * *

People at the office can see that I do not have any work. To save myself this embarrassment, I ask the manager for something to do. She has promised me a project that is in the pipeline. For now, she gives me a list of clients. I am to amend their contact details. I call them, asking if their details have changed. When speaking, I am conscious of my voice. I would rather the people around me did not hear.

* * *

I continue looking for accommodation on Gumtree. There are so many prohibitions: only females need apply, only Muslim males, only white males, only Christian guys, smokers not welcome. I jot down the few places that are suitable for me. I am learning how difficult it is to find accommodation in Cape Town. Time is running out. There is a room available in a two-bedroom flat in Vredehoek leased by a woman. It is open to both guys and girls. She is keen on an easy-going, fun-loving flatmate. I arrange to view the place after work. I have never been to Vredehoek before. The woman tells me that the taxis are around the KFC on Shortmarket Street. The taxi struggles up Buitenkant Street to a block of flats at the foot of the mountain. I know the woman. Her name is Chantel. She also did business science at UCT, and at some point she stayed in my sister residence, though I never said a word to her when we were still studying. She is doing well, works at a bank, has a car. The flat is impressive, the lounge is spacious and the room is furnished. But the rent is steep at two thousand seven hundred rand a month and the location is inconvenient. I would have preferred somewhere in the southern suburbs. Because I am desperate, I agree to pay her the deposit the next day.

* * *

The office becomes fervent on payday. More enhanced than the Friday joy. Smiles come more easily. It's a contrast to Monday mornings, when people are usually gloomy. I pay Chantel the money for the deposit, and eighteen hundred rand to ABSA for my student loan. I have about three thousand rand left.

I buy *The Artist's Way* from a second-hand shop in town for ninety-nine rand. It speaks of a Creator who wants us to be creative and takes pleasure in such efforts. I do the exercises from the book in my room. I remember that I used to be able to draw well but was discouraged at school when a friend took an impromptu sketch I had made and showed it around, saying how terrible it was. Since then, I haven't drawn. In the book they encourage the writing of morning pages each day to clear the emotional clutter in the psyche. Anger comes to me one morning while doing my morning pages – anger at Nhlakanipho, for mocking me for not becoming an accountant, and at Mpumelelo, for removing my panama. I have never been able to stand up to Nhlakanipho. He has done so much to me, like not returning money or books that I lent him.

I call Nhlakanipho from work one afternoon. "I did not like what you said to me that Saturday evening at your place," I say, overcoming the nerves.

"What did I do?" Nhlakanipho asks with an innocent ring in his voice.

"I felt you were spiteful when you said that Zandi used to say I was going to be an accountant," I tell Nhlakanipho. He says he was only joking.

Later in the afternoon I receive a message from Nhlakanipho: "Manga, I still don't get what you are upset about. But if I offended you, I am sorry."

I give in to the wave of apologies and reply: "Maybe I was wrong."

"Hayi, dude, you were," Nhlakanipho retorts.

* * *

For one year we all stayed at Liesbeeck Gardens residence: Nhlakanipho, Tongai and I. Early one morning, Nhlakanipho knocked, punching at my door. He had a pair of scissors in his right hand.

"Look at me," he said. His face was swollen, his left eye closed.

"Is this my fault?" I stuttered.

I was convinced he was going to stab me. To my relief, he shook his head, stuck his tongue out and walked away.

Nhlakanipho had been beaten up at a party in one of the residences. I saw him catching a punch; as big as he was, he fell to the ground. I mediated, pacifying the brothers who were attacking him. We stood with Nhlakanipho against a wall far from the scene. Then Nhlakanipho started breaking beer bottles; I was startled, did not know what to do. He walked up to those guys with a broken bottle, shouting, "Which one of you am I going to kill?" They beckoned to him with bottles of their own. Nhlakanipho ran towards them. Then he was lying on the ground with the group of men stomping on him.

When I asked Nhlakanipho the following day about coming to my room carrying a pair of scissors, he said he did not remember it.

* * *

From the veins in my arms, I thirst for beer. On Fridays we are allowed to come to work in casual gear. From the office, I go straight to Roots in Lower Main Road, Observatory, too eager even to drop off my backpack at home. I down a flurry of beers until my blood settles. There are some brothers smoking zol at another table. By now my head is buzzing. I step up to these guys and wait for my turn on the joint. I take a few drags and return to my table. On some occasions I am good on my own. People just seem to disturb me. Alcohol puts me in a reflective, reminiscent mood. My thoughts are sweet.

Rasun joins me in the starry night. He has soft dreadlocks made from knotting together straight hair. I keep dozing off on the table.

"Did you eat before drinking?" Rasun asks.

I shake my head.

"Fuck, you are fucking yourself up," Rasun says.

Rasun wants us to hunt for women. I am not in a good state to accompany him. He gets irritated with me as I keep switching off, almost passing out. I met Rasun through hip-hop. He heard a track I had recorded with some guys back in varsity. Since then he was adamant that we should be friends. He is awkward around people, the result of bipolar disorder. I like his craziness, though; with him I can laugh about the absurd. He leaves me in a fit of rage, cursing me for being too drunk. My intestines grumble and my mouth is full of spittle as I watch him stalk out of Roots.

*   *   *

On Saturday afternoon, feeling lonely, I cruise the streets of Observatory. I carry my bloated stomach to Obzone. There is loud music blaring upstairs. One gentleman gets on the mic to announce the next act. I share a joint with Moses on the balcony. He has a camera with him and tells me that he studied at AFDA and stays in Gugulethu. We exchange numbers. The live band transfixes me; the vocalist howls to crawling children, shatters glass when she raises her voice. Then I travel with the horns, the trumpets and saxophones to an eternal wilderness.

*   *   *

I get up well into the next day, my mouth black from smoking. I want to stop drinking more than I want to stop smoking. My belly has expanded from drinking every weekend. I have stretch marks around my lower back. But on Fridays I cannot control the urge. Regret floods me on my sorrowful Sundays. Then I start the week promising myself not to touch any alcohol.

*   *   *

I have been calling Noziqhamo since the day she gave me her number, but our work schedules clash. One afternoon she gets off work early. We agree to meet at Salt River station. I cut work and leave my backpack under my desk. They will not notice my absence from the office. There have been times when I have not shown up and no one has asked me anything.

I find Noziqhamo on a bench. She smiles when she sees me.

"Did you leave work early?" she asks.

"Don't worry about that, I work on my own time," I reply.

We walk through industrial Salt River to my place. On one wall there is a piece of graffiti: "People over profit." None of my house-mates are at home. I lead Noziqhamo to my room. I sit on my bed while she fills the chair, her knees bent, feet on the seat.

"You seem young," Noziqhamo observes.

"How old do you think I am?" I ask.

"Younger than twenty-six," she answers.

"I am twenty-four."

"You are too young. What will people say when they see me walking with you in the street?"

"How old are you?" I ask.

"Over thirty."

"Wow, you do not look that old."

"I am."

Noziqhamo says she has a three-year-old son. I confess to having children of my own. You rushed things, Noziqhamo says. Her baby's father died in a car accident. Later I retract my lie about being a father. I look at Noziqhamo. Her legs are apart. I swallow sweet juices. Still in my work clothes, I walk towards her and start swinging between her thighs. She starts to moan, and kisses me back when I slide my tongue into her mouth.

"Don't do this, you are going to hurt yourself," Noziqhamo cautions as I continue swinging between her jeans.

I carry her to my bed. On top of her jeans, I pound, faster, until I ejaculate in my underwear. I wipe the drops of sweat off my forehead. I walk Noziqhamo back to the station and keep her company while she waits for a train.

*　*　*

The days pile up at the office, still with no project for me. The manager is brusque. We barely speak, save for nodding and greeting each other when our paths cross. With nothing to do at work, I have resorted to reading. I pass the time by going through a motivational book about thinking big that a colleague has given me. In a quiet moment I see dusty children playing on a street teeming with life, young girls skipping rope. I have been barred from going out because I have sore tonsils. This is my view from the window for my creative writing assignment.

My piece is the shortest. The instructor likes it. She likes my direct style of writing. "You must not change your style of writing," she advises. One woman writes in a beautiful lyrical language; she pulsates rhythms with yellow words. The instructor faults her for overstating things. For an entire paragraph she describes the weather.

*　*　*

Nhlakanipho called me one evening and announced that he had found a job.

"Nice, congratulations," I said.

Nhlakanipho said they were out having drinks with Tongai. "I won't be able to make it," I said.

I did not have the verve to be happy with Nhlakanipho. Tongai began working a year before me and Nhlakanipho. They went to pubs together, spending Tongai's earnings. Nhlakanipho always related more with Tongai. I struggled with Tongai; on two occasions he called me a funny character. Only later did I seethe, thinking of the disrespect.

*　*　*

I move to Vredehoek on a Sunday afternoon. A housemate drives me up, the sun high in the sky. The road through Vredehoek is dauntingly steep. The wind blows hard, pushing on my face, tugging at my clothes. Chantel is standing in the lounge with the window open, smoking a cigarette. She has a white beanie on. I place my bag in my room.

*　*　*

I do not have a desk in my room, so I use the one in the lounge for writing in my journal. I look up and see Chantel walking in from behind.

"Don't tell me you keep a diary," she remarks, on her way to the kitchen.

"No . . . it's not a diary," I say, looking at the page.

"Then what is it?"

"It's a stream of consciousness. Whatever is on my mind, I write about it."

There is a faint smell of cigarette smoke coming from Chantel's room. She heats her Weet-Bix in the microwave. Her sense of dress is effortless: long black pants and a plain white blouse. She drives a grey Corsa. I wait for a taxi outside our block of flats. The minibus is filled mostly by black women who work in Vredehoek. This is no conventional taxi route; anyone gets picked up along the way. We pay five rand to get to town.

*   *   *

In my plentiful idle time at the office, I apply for vacancies I see on the internet. An asset management company gets back to me regarding a position as an intern. The job is more in line with what I studied at university. I arrange for the interview to take place during lunchtime. I do my research about the company, which was formed by some black guys after they left a predominantly white corporate behemoth.

On the day of my interview, I wait in the reception area of the company. The receptionist tells me to go through to the boardroom. Two partners, an accountant and a senior researcher, sit at a rectangular table. I sit on the short side of the table, facing one of the partners.

"Your marks are good," the accountant says, looking at my transcript. "But . . . then . . . what happened at the postgraduate diploma? You failed just about every course?"

"I got tired of accounting. It was not what I wanted . . . my failing was not a case of a lack of ability," I say.

"This does not look good, starting something and not finishing it," the researcher adds.

"Accounting is not what I wanted to do."

"Do you think accounting is not relevant to this job?" he asks.

Now in a corner, I keep quiet.

"You are currently working at Trilce Health," the accountant remarks.

"Ja, I want to leave. The programme is not well structured, there isn't work for us graduates."

He nods thoughtfully.

"Why do you want to work for this company?"

"I researched how it was started . . ." I hold myself back from saying "by black guys". "This company is more related to my field – finance."

"It seems like you do not know what you want," the accountant says.

"Do we ever?" I say softly.

"Look, you speak well and you look smart, but that does not count for anything. You must stick it out at Trilce, even if it means being a skivvy. Appreciate that you are getting advice from successful people."

I get out of there and buy a cigarette in the street. I inhale the smoke and blow out the arrogance of the wealthy.

* * *

One Saturday evening, Mfundo's place was full of women in shining make-up and expensive jeans. They all worked in retail outlets.

"There's your man, Nthabiseng," Mpumelelo said as I walked into the flat. "She's forever asking about you, Manga."

I kept quiet and sat down.

The other women were part of Mfundo's syndicate. They specialised in getting credit card details from customers. They spoke highly of Mfundo.

"I have known Mfundo for eight years," one woman said.

"Keep quiet, listen!" Mfundo ordered us, lining up cocaine with a credit card.

"I have known Mfundo for eight years," continued the woman. "I am thirty now, neh. He has been so good to us. He stepped in when my boyfriend was giving me trouble. See, Mfundo, he did not even have to go into this life, his parents left him a big house with a swimming pool in Langa. He's sweet, Mfundo, but don't take advantage. All it takes is one bullet, just one bullet."

There were gold bottles of champagne on the glass coffee table. Mfundo danced to house music, his head swaying. We heard a scream from outside. Nhlakanipho and I went to check. Nthabiseng was in tears, crying: "I'm going home, Mpumi." Mpumelelo dragged her by the arm upstairs to his flat.

*   *   *

I felt as empty as a beer bottle the Sunday after the drinking and cocaine. Outside, the sun was a yellow eye on the face of the blue sky. During my lunch breaks at work, I had been bumping into a shaven, pony-tailed Hare Krishna devotee. He had given me a handout with directions to a temple in Rondebosch. I just needed a sense of closure. I do not believe in the sanctity of the religion.

I took off my shoes before entering the place of worship. The believers knelt in front of a statue of Prabhupada, and then sat in a circle on the floor. They chanted, gyrating, with the drums beating, and kept pushing a black man into the circle. His eyes wide open, he jumped to please them. They clapped euphorically.

I came out of there feeling hazy. There was something sedative about the Hare Krishna energy and their food.

*   *   *

Nhlakanipho and I e-mail each other from our workplaces. He tells me about the drama that unfolded between Nthabiseng and Mpumelelo in the wee hours of Sunday morning. Mpumelelo beat Nthabiseng, saying he wanted her to shit her insides out. Nhlakanipho had to come between them.

* * *

One Saturday afternoon Nhlakanipho came to visit me in Vrede-hoek. He wore a grey top and looked sombre.

"I don't know what to do with Mpumi," he confided. "He keeps on fighting with Nthabiseng. I don't even know why he's still with this chick. How can you be with someone who lied to you about being pregnant? She also sleeps around. People in Clare-mont know she's a slut. I don't think I would even like Mpumi if he was not family," Nhlakanipho said, looking down. Tears were rising in his eyes.

"He comes in and makes sweeping statements, saying I'm self-ish. He does not encourage me in any way. Mpumi . . . he's not even working a legit job. That call centre of theirs is a pyramid scheme; they keep changing the name of the company. I don't think we should be staying together. I am better off on my own. It was fine when we were younger."

"This is beyond me, beyond us, it needs someone older," I ad-vised.

"Do you think Mpumi will listen to anyone? He's a raging bull in that house."

Nhlakanipho shakes his head. The crying makes me uncom-fortable. I don't know how to comfort a guy my age. Nhlakanipho says Mfundo is recruiting us. I wouldn't mind cutting a deal and making a couple of thousand, I tell him.

"Mfundo has made a lot of people rich," Nhlakanipho says. "A lot of prominent people like him for that."

* * *

In the early morning, as we prepare for work, Chantel storms out of her room.

"Magasiso, could you please clean the stove after cooking," she yells, not even saying my name right. "Look at this, it is disgusting," she says pointing at the grease around the hotplate. "And the lights, you are wasting electricity, switch them off at night," she chides, looking at me. I remain silent a while, nod and say, "OK".

I am slow-tempered. Later, at the office, I think of what Chantel said. It was disrespectful. It's not that I mind being told off; it's just the tone of her voice that I did not like. I have to learn to stand up for myself.

I get back to the flat before Chantel. For a while I watch TV.

"Don't tell me you are one of those Oprah fans," Chantel says as she sits down next to me.

"No, I'm not a fan."

"Then why are you watching?"

"Just passing time."

I have been trying to chat with Chantel in the time that I have been staying with her, but she is hard to get through to. She keeps a stern wall between us. I muster the courage to confront her.

"About this morning. I did not like how you spoke to me. It's not you complaining about my cleanliness. I just did not like the tone of your voice."

"Then how do you want me to talk to you?" Chantel raises her voice.

"Not like that . . . you could soften your voice . . . Rather don't talk to me if that's how you gonna talk," I say. She sticks her tongue out at me and goes to her room.

* * *

Chantel brings a dark-skinned man to the apartment one evening. She is wearing denim shorts. I watch her bending as she closes the curtains in the lounge where I am watching TV. She offers him Coke to drink. I have never seen her make a courteous gesture. Later, they play music loud to hide their lovemaking noises.

* * *

A training workshop frees me from the office for a week. All the graduates from my year assemble on the twenty-second floor of the Trilce headquarters. First, we have to fill in a questionnaire about how we would react to different work scenarios. Then we are each given a bar chart with different colours for various personality types (red for competitive, blue for thinker, yellow for sociable and green for passive do-gooder). My chart is predominantly blue and green; the blue means that I am a thinking introvert, while the green indicates someone who is earthy and conflict-averse. A comment on the side reads: "Don't be deceived by Mangaliso's reticent look; he will look for ingenious ways to make himself invisible." They say I have an ability to form long-lasting friendships with strange characters.

I become sour as the workshop drags on. *All this to make us more productive, taking away the colour from people.* I think of Kwanele, who hates psychometric tests. He sees them as a means to control employees more effectively. Friday comes and closes the curtain on a draining week.

* * *

My eyes go straight to Noziqhamo's upper thighs. She is standing in front of the Chicken Licken at the station deck taxi rank. There

81

is something curvy but also athletic about her physique. Her hips round her thighs in a healthy portion and yet she is slim. Before coming down to meet her, I bought biscuits, cold drink and a packet of condoms. We drive up to my flat in a taxi. The heat in my room is searing. We kiss on the bed, Noziqhamo's tongue wiggling clumsily in my mouth. I try taking off her jeans.

"No, no, Mangaliso . . . This is a sin in front of God's eyes," she says.

"Oh, come on," I say, my erection visible to her.

"Are you too horny? . . . Do you just want to come? . . . Can't you do me on top of my panties?"

"I have some condoms," I reply, shaking my head.

"I know you boys . . . you always have condoms."

"Are you not gonna give it to me, then?"

"The Bible says ask and it shall be given to you," Noziqhamo says, lifting her upper lip slightly.

"Please, Noziqhamo."

* * *

I ejaculate. Noziqhamo continues thrusting her hips on my fading erection. She pushes up twice and throws her arms around me, moaning my name. Afterwards, I watch her succulent buttocks as she puts on her green panties.

* * *

Noziqhamo always has a runny nose. The last time she was with me she kept on blowing her nose. I do not believe that her baby's father died in a car accident. It could have been AIDS. Over the phone, she tells me that she has a terrible fever, and is feeling hot and cold. She has not been well for close to a month.

She came to see me one Saturday. By now she knew the way to my place. It was not cold, yet she had on a heavy layered jacket. She took coy nibbles of the biscuits I had given her. She had lost a lot of weight. I rubbed her thigh; under her jeans she had long black tights on, and yet the jeans were still loose.

"No, there's something . . ." Noziqhamo said when I tried pulling down her tights. "I'm on my period."

"It does not matter," I said, the juices in my throat now.

"You don't mind even if there's blood?" she asked, pointing with her index and middle finger together.

"No," I replied.

I rolled a condom over my erect penis. When I pulled out of her, the soaked condom was red around the tip. I flushed it down the toilet. I returned to find Noziqhamo still naked, her face buried in her knees. She was coughing hard, the heaving accentuating the outline of her spine. After walking Noziqhamo to the taxi, I sat in a bar in town, satisfied, with a beer and a cigarette.

* * *

Chantel shouts out my name while I am lying in bed one evening. I go to her. She is standing in front of the toilet.

"Dude, if you gonna piss on the floor . . . you must clean up," she yells.

I go closer to the loo. There are drops of urine in front of the bowl. I wipe the floor with a spaghetti mop.

* * *

I skirt around my manager's office. She is hardly ever in. Time at work is a shame. I cannot hide my idle hands. From the other graduates, I hear that there is a manager in another department looking for graduates. The manager in question was also in the graduate programme. I send him an e-mail. He replies, requests my CV and asks me to explain what I have been doing since I started working at Trilce. In the space of two days I prepare the required documents and mail them to him, as requested. He asks to see me. I walk up to his office on the afternoon of our meeting. The manager is a tall coloured man not more than three years my senior. He offers me the position of technical specialist. The logistics of communicating with my current manager he will handle himself. I have to see out the month before taking up the vacancy.

* * *

There are paintings in the galleries on Long Street. I visit one of these galleries during my lunch break. The owner is an Indian. He sells portraits of primitive African women and of Bushmen. *They are peddling a preconceived idea of Africa. This is not true art.* I get hold of a copy of *Hard Times* by Charles Dickens from a second-hand bookshop. Such a neat and concise use of language I have not seen before.

* * *

The poem comes to me on a lonely Friday night. I think of my father. Does he know that I lost my virginity to a slippery mother? Or that I bedded women who reeked of halitosis and had poisonous pussies? The poem I title "Paternal Transmission". As I wrestle with the feeling, referring to the dictionary for the right words, Chantel walks in with two of her friends. They are carrying boxed wine. Chantel introduces me.

"What are you doing?" one of her friends asks.

84

"Just watching TV . . . and also trying to write," I mumble.

"Watching TV on a Friday night," she says.

I nod, laughing quietly.

They take the party to Chantel's room. I hear them roaring with laughter behind the closed door. *People have even become covetous of laughter these days.* Chantel comes out to clean a hubbly-bubbly in the kitchen sink. She goes back to the room. I smell the scent of marijuana.

* * *

I drive with Rasun to Gugulethu. There's a hip-hop gig at the sports complex this Sunday morning. Moses told me about the event. He rents a shack made of corrugated iron in someone's yard, but says there's too much noise. He has weed wrapped in a newspaper in his shack. Moses rolls a joint and we blaze. Rasun does not smoke ganja any more. With my eyes narrowed by the effect of the weed, we make our way to the sports complex.

Hip-hop cats from across the Cape Flats are scattered on the basketball courts. They circle around in their crews. There's an effort with the clothing: skater tackies, complex headgear. In every corner a joint is burning. They shoot with words on the mic, giving intense performances. One lady emcee holds the time. She moves like a praise singer of old, beating with her tongue men who rape and abuse. This is beauty, seeing young people express themselves so passionately.

* * *

I pack up the little that I have from my cubicle and say goodbye to the woman who sits next to me. She wishes me good luck for the future.

I have a team in my new department. There is a clear function for me: to compile reports. In my first two weeks on the floor I go through the preparation of the reports with the woman who was previously responsible for this function. She will now focus on her actual work.

They ask me my clan name at the office. The men are referred to by their clan names. I give them my mother's.

I struggle with the reports at first. The manager chides me for submitting erroneous results. My young manager asserts his authority. With more time, I master the preparation of these reports. The manager only acknowledges the timely submissions.

*   *   *

I visited Nhlakanipho one Friday evening. I found him drunk and drooling on the couch, gulping the last bits of a nip of brandy. His speech was slurred, but he still managed to jab me, accusing me of not taking him seriously and thinking him a joke. Mpumelelo came out of his room with Nthabiseng. He horsed around with Nhlakanipho, shaking his hand. Mpumelelo seemed to enjoy seeing Nhlakanipho out of sorts. From a brown envelope, Mpumelelo took out some weed he had bought at the taxi rank, and rolled a joint. It gave me only a weak high. I left Nhlakanipho passed out on the couch and caught a bus to town. I drank at a bar just to calm the urge.

I was surprised to get a call from Nthabiseng, as we had never exchanged numbers before. She asked to see me and directed me to her place. I finished my beer and went to the taxi rank. I was nervous, not knowing what to expect from her. There was a cold wind ruffling the trees as I walked past the bus terminus in Mowbray to a commune opposite Liesbeeck Gardens. I found Nthabiseng wearing pyjamas and a gown; her face was red and her upper lip was swollen.

"I don't know why I'm telling you this," Nthabiseng said, looking down. Her right leg was crossed over her left. "Mpumelelo attacked me tonight. He beats me a lot . . ."

I looked at Nthabiseng. Strands of hair covered her face.

"He beats me all the time," she said, and started sobbing. "I was pregnant with his child last year. I just couldn't go through with it. I aborted the child in Joburg. I just couldn't have a child with Mpumelelo." Nthabiseng rubbed her eyes after saying this.

She went to the kitchen and came back with a bottle of wine. She poured for both of us. The bottle was half-empty. She had been drinking before I came.

I spent the night in Nthabiseng's bed. She cried as we made love and I tasted her tears. I hurried out of the apartment in the morning, looking for any hint of Mpumelelo.

We did not use a condom. For the next few weeks I counted the days, worried that she might be pregnant. Despite everything, her relationship with Mpumelelo continued. I realised that she needed him for everything, to stand. She was not able to do it alone. Before meeting Mpumelelo, she had no friends and wandered on her own around Cape Town.

* * *

My ears are clogged. I have a gripping cold and sore throat. I go through rolls of toilet paper blowing my nose. But I decide to visit Moses in Gugulethu. It is a public holiday. I take drags from a cigarette at the taxi rank in town, aggravating my sore throat. I get off close to Zingisa Primary School in NY1 in Gugulethu. There is a billboard on the school grounds advertising toothpaste. In front of me is an enclave with women cooking meat and two white shelters with phone booths. I keep looking across the street, waiting for Moses.

When he comes, we walk down the tarred road. The streets in Gugulethu are narrow. Some youths are standing in front of a run-down cream building.

"I have family that live here," Moses says, pointing at the building.

Moses' shack is made of wood and corrugated iron. It does not stand properly, and instead leans to one side.

Moses is bitter, aggrieved about how people are living. He does not see any hope, even with the upcoming World Cup.

"The only people that will benefit are FIFA," Moses says.

His passion is film. He and a few other township brothers are hustling a production company. Moses lights up when he tells me of their plans. They want to shoot township stories right in Gugulethu. Moses has a thick book on scriptwriting next to his computer. He also makes beats and we freestyle over the music after smoking a joint.

Moses suggests we go buy some fish in Heideveld. I'm all for the idea, as the weed has made me hungry. Heideveld is a township of coloured and black people, a few streets from Gugulethu.

Moses has been a good host. He has entertained and fed me. He accompanies me to the taxi rank in Nyanga. I get off in town in the early evening, and am lucky to catch the last taxi to Vredehoek. If I had missed it, I would have had to pay for a meter cab. The taxi slows down on the blue asphalt before dropping me in front of our block of flats.

My ears are severely blocked. I try forcing them open by pushing air through my nose. My left eardrum vibrates. I lose balance and lean against the wall in my room. I struggle to walk to the lounge. At night, as I lie in bed, I position my head on the pillow so as to try to curb the dizziness.

* * *

I cannot go to work the next morning. I send my manager a message, informing him of my illness.

"It's fine, just make sure you bring a doctor's note," he replies.

It gets worse. When I try getting out of bed, I fall on the floor. My head is not steady. I crawl to the bathroom. I do not eat for the whole day. I sleep with my right ear pressed against the pillow.

* * *

I have a problem the next day. I am running out of water. This could lead to death. I can barely move in bed; the slightest movement makes my head spin wildly. I have vomited on the floor a few times. I crawl to the corridor, shouting "Somebody help!", lying on my stomach on the carpet. Somehow I manage to reach up and open the front door. An old white man comes out of his flat. "What's wrong?" he asks. I explain to him that I stay in the flat with the open door and that my ear is buzzing; I cannot even stand. He goes into his flat and brings back a glass of water. A few minutes after drinking the water, I feel nauseous. I writhe to the bathroom and puke.

A woman finds us, me still on the floor, the old man standing above me. I tell her my condition. She suspects I have burst an eardrum and says I have to go to the hospital.

"Are you on medical aid?" the old man asks.

"No, I'm not," I reply.

"Well, who's going to pay for the ambulance?" the man asks.

"I'm fucking dying here . . . and you're asking me about that."

The woman says she has burst an eardrum before. There's nothing the doctors can really do besides giving you a course of antibiotics. She leaves, saying she has work to do. She hopes I get better. One of the security guards who works in the building comes to my rescue. He calls an ambulance and waits with me.

After about an hour, the green-clad ambulance personnel arrive. They check my blood pressure and carry me down in a stretcher to the ambulance. From Vredehoek the closest hospital is Somerset, in Green Point. A paramedic sits with me in the back of the ambulance. She is gentle, and I start falling in love with her. At two o'clock we are told that Somerset is closed, so we make our way to Groote Schuur. I observe the other patients from the stretcher as we enter the hospital.

I am carried to the waiting room. They lift me off the stretcher and onto a trolley. I look around; there are plenty of people in here. Some are accompanied by their relatives, who sit on the benches.

After a few hours in the waiting room, a woman arrives with her pregnant daughter. She sits to my right, and says I do not look sick.

"Do you go to church?" she asks.

"No, I don't go to church."

"No one is meant to be sick . . . You do not look sick to me at all . . . It could be evil spirits that are attacking you."

My skin shivers at the thought of this.

A man wearing a black suit walks into the waiting room. "If you are a believer in Jesus Christ, please close your eyes and pray with me," he announces. I do not believe in God but, nonetheless, I close my eyes and pray.

It is only at nine in the evening that I get to see the doctor. A male nurse pushes me in a wheelchair to the doctor's room. A young white trainee doctor assists. She is quick to suggest I take an AIDS test. The doctor reprimands her with a fierce look.

They say my left ear is more inflamed than my right one. Still, they are unsure. They speculate it could be jaundice. The trainee doctor draws blood from me for testing. With no immediate danger to my health, they discharge me and set up an appointment with an ear specialist.

Because it is late, I spend the night at the hospital. The patient next to me coughs a harrowing cough throughout the night. His exposed chest is bony; he looks like death and smells horrific. The nurses mock him, asking him how many girlfriends he has had. In the morning, they find he has pissed himself, and one nurse hurls insults at him.

I send a message to Chantel, asking her to pick me up. She does not reply. I call her and she does not pick up her phone. I have to leave the hospital before nine o'clock. An old friend helps me out. He agrees to fetch me from the hospital. He comes into the ward not more than thirty minutes after I phone him. I am surprised that I am able to get up from bed and sit in the wheelchair without any assistance. I leave the hospital with a note for the appointment with the ear specialist. My friend gets my medication from the dispensary.

* * *

Chantel comes to my room and explains that she was asleep when I called. She even goes out and gets me some bananas.

* * *

91

On the day of my appointment with the ear specialist, I make my way to Groote Schuur early in the morning. I am completely healed now and my balance is restored. I wait in line at the hospital. Before seeing the specialist, I need to first have my folder, a nurse tells me. I request my folder at the reception area. I'm asked to join an immense line. For close to four hours, I wait for my turn. When I reach the front of the line, they do not have my folder. They send me on a run-around for the next two hours, but they cannot locate my folder. I give up on seeing the specialist and settle for a doctor's note.

On my return to the office, I hand my manager the medical note. He looks at it, infers that I must have had an ear infection, and continues with his work.

* * *

Chantel calls me from my room late one Friday afternoon. She is seething about the piss on the bathroom floor.

"Dude, how old are you?" Chantel asks with disdain, wrinkling her cheeks. "You are twenty-five years old. What's wrong with you? Can't you aim?" she cries. "You are worse than a pig. Not even animals behave like this!"

I ask her to show me the piss. I struggle to see anything. She points to three drops of urine on the floor, saying I'm also blind.

"There's something wrong with you," I burst out, not able to contain myself any longer. "You have demons of your own."

"Are you completely out of your mind? I'm not the one pissing on the floor! I have friends. I have business science. I have a good job. I have a car," Chantel says to me.

"There's something wrong, the mere fact that you have to tell me that," I reply.

"You think you are so smart; you are actually just dumb," Chantel says and walks to her room.

I do not know what to make of all this. I could be the one in the wrong. I set my jaw and wet the mop in the sink. This place has never felt like home. I am constantly uncomfortable. I feel uneasy when Chantel walks in from work and I am eating in the lounge.

After cleaning the toilet, I leave the flat and catch a taxi to town. The only comfort I know is beer. At La Reference I drink a Black Label quart from the bottle. It is dim in the bar; La Reference is cheap compared to other places on Long Street.

An Indian woman comes up to me. She wastes no time. "You are very handsome, can you buy me a beer?" she asks. I suggest she get a glass and we share the beer.

This woman has dark patches below her eyes. I can tell she takes drugs. Also, she is not attractive. She follows me into the smoking section. There are four women sitting here. One woman chases the Indian out as soon as she lays eyes on her. *This is some territorial fight between prostitutes.* One of the women suggests I join them.

Anita is telling a story. One night she was smoking crack in a room after her work in the street was done. In the bed, a young boy was savagely fucking some girl. For more than four rounds, he did not even change the condom, Anita says.

"Yoh, AIDS, they are going to die," a stout woman says, looking into a mirror and applying lipstick.

"You . . . have you ever had makwerekwere pussy?" she asks, looking at me.

I shake my head, looking down.

"It's like nothing you've ever had. We can get a room upstairs."

I develop an erection, but still shake my head.

The others leave me with Anita, saying they're off to business. We share beers. Anita tells me her life story, of the streets of Hillbrow, smoking so much crack, turning into a zombie and coming back home to Gugulethu. She says she has a daughter. I do not know whether this is some ploy she uses on clients who fit my description. She gives me her number when I leave her. At the entrance to La Reference stands the woman who offered me pussy.

"I thought you were with my friend?" she remarks.

"No, I left her inside," I respond.

* * *

News from the Cape Flats reaches my ears at the office: robberies, housebreakings in which the husband and wife are raped, flashy rich gangsters. Credit card fraud is increasing. My colleagues share tips about the most effective burglar systems and alarms. Keeping an illegal firearm is a means of protection for some working people. One man in my team admits to owning an unlicensed gun. He says it is better than having a legal one: you can shoot a robber without having to deal with the fingers of the law.

* * *

A dark cloud descended on me after Nhlakanipho told me Mfundo had been arrested for assaulting his girlfriend. He stabbed her seven times with a knife, then broke a broom and stabbed her with that. There were pools of blood, and even pieces of bone, in Mfundo's flat. Nhlakanipho said Mfundo was in Pollsmoor.

A couple of weeks later, Nhlakanipho announced that Mfundo was out of jail. Mfundo spent his first night out with Mpumelelo.

They drank a bottle of Jack Daniel's and snorted cocaine. Mfundo believed it was the ancestors that made him butcher his girl-friend. In the weekend that Mfundo was arrested, three of his friends were shot and killed. It was the aftermath of the war Mfundo had told us about. His girlfriend, the mother of his daughter, survived and was eventually discharged from hospital.

* * *

One Saturday afternoon Nhlakanipho told me that he was at Springbok's in Newlands. I found him sitting with Mfundo at one of the wooden tables. Springbok's was quite empty. Mfundo was clean-shaven and dressed in expensive-looking clothing. I noticed a scar on the back of his head. Tongai was also there, nodding and bowing to the swings of conversation. Mpumelelo raced with Mfundo, quickly switching gears as if to prove he was also streetwise. I had developed a fear of Mfundo. If he could do that to the mother of his child, he could also do it to us.

There was a Stormers game at Newlands Stadium. As we walked along Boundary Road, a man offered us tickets at a reduced price. Mfundo took up the offer, and carried into the ground a placard on which was written "Ek is 'n Stormer". The four of us sat high up in the stands to watch the game. It was a family outing, with children and parents all wearing Stormers jerseys. Mfundo was on the phone throughout the match, laughing with his friends. After the game, Nhlakanipho hugged Mfundo, thanking him for getting us tickets. Later, Nhlakanipho confided to me that he wanted to cry; no one had ever done that for him. He said he felt like Tupac, who cried after attending an NBA game for the first time.

* * *

Chantel corners me one evening, entering my room without bothering to knock. With her hands on her hips, she says she can't stand staying with me any more.

"I have never stayed with someone who pisses on the floor," she says, looking at the open window. "This room smells like someone died here three months ago."

"Three months ago," I repeat.

"Yes, the time you have been here."

Anger rises in my throat. I get up. I have taken more than enough shit from Chantel. I do not have the might or the mind to speak right now. But Chantel would certainly have me arrested were I to slap her. I restrain myself, mutter some Xhosa curses.

Chantel gives me a month's notice to find a new place. The previous tenant also did not leave Chantel on good terms. Perhaps a bachelor flat would suit me better. At the commune I struggled with my housemates. There was the guy who was always on my case, even complaining about me not washing the dishes properly. But bachelor apartments in the southern suburbs are way out of my reach. I would have to pay at least three and a half thousand rand a month. I'm not familiar with the northern suburbs; moving there would take me out of my circle of friends. An extra job from Mfundo could come in handy to raise money for a deposit. Despite all the speculation that Mfundo was recruiting us, he has not made any concrete offers, and, in fact, discouraged Mpumelelo when he asked for hook-ups.

"Do you think I enjoy doing this, having to change cars for reasons of safety?" Mfundo said. He says he was once told by a doctor that he had a brain tumour and had six months to live. He asked the doctor to discharge him and went deeper into gangsterism. Now he cannot get out of it.

Mpumelelo thinks that Mfundo is running out of money. He and Nhlakanipho amuse themselves over the prospect of Mfundo's demise.

"He cannot blame us for spending his money. When we met he did not have that much money left," Mpumelelo says.

*   *   *

One Sunday, Mfundo has a young prostitute with him in his apartment. He confesses that it is a dry season; Nhlakanipho has paid for the cocaine and champagne today.

Nthabiseng is extra-friendly with Mfundo. She taps Mfundo's shoulder when she laughs. When Nthabiseng goes to the bathroom, Mfundo beckons to Mpumelelo. "Tell your bitch to get off my dick," he says in Mpumelelo's ear.

Mfundo is losing his ability to speak English. He often gets stuck in sentences and throws in a Xhosa word. When he is with us, Mfundo wants to converse in English. Nhlakanipho cannot afford the champagne that Mfundo usually buys. With only two grams of cocaine available, Mfundo scoops for us sparingly. Nhlakanipho recalls how he came to UCT from high school, and how he worked hard and made it into the top ten in matric.

"I did it all to correct Mpumi's slip-up of failing grade eleven," he says.

Mpumelelo does not seem to like this recollection. Nhlakanipho does not notice and instead sinks deeper into his skin.

"I'm only twenty-four years old," Nhlakanipho says. "Mandela was also twenty-four when he said he was going to be the future president of the ANC."

Nhlakanipho quickly fills his glass. Whenever we drink, he wants to consume the most alcohol. He usually looks for the biggest glass and then ends the night being a nuisance to us by passing out.

"Just because you bought the drinks . . . you don't have to drink with greed," Mpumelelo chastises Nhlakanipho.

Mpumelelo sizzles with bitterness for the rest of the day. He keeps saying that Nhlakanipho and I are just laaities.

"I think it was God that brought Mfundo to us," Nhlakanipho continues in his majestic tirade.

This pleases Mfundo, but his smile fades when I look at him.

"I don't know how else to explain his coming into our lives."

It is surprising seeing Nthabiseng snort cocaine. She bends her head and sniffs up like an expert. We haven't spoken since the night we slept together. When I walked into the flat, she greeted me the same way she usually does. Nthabiseng is wearing a denim skirt. Her legs are crossed as she sits on Mfundo's leather couch.

"These are my friends . . . guys like Manga," Nhlakanipho says. "These are the people who know me. They know my strengths and my weaknesses. If we were to be enemies, we would be ruthless e-ne-mies," drawing out the syllables for effect.

"But Manga, you would never be enemies with Nhlakanipho," Mfundo says.

"You never know, you can never fully know what lies in a man's heart," I say. This is followed by silence.

I see a megalomaniac in Nhlakanipho. His view of the world revolves around his ego. When his ego is bruised, he gossips about people. I'm certain that he speaks about me behind my back. He does the same with Tongai and Mpumelelo when they are not around. Nhlakanipho undermines my and Tongai's ambitions of being writers, seeing us as giving up, having lost all hope of attaining real success.

I refill my glass with champagne. I smoke non-stop when I drink. It's not even for the pleasure any more, but rather just to feel a cigarette in my mouth.

"How long are you gonna work at a call centre?" Mfundo lashes out at Mpumelelo.

Mpumelelo and Mfundo have a brutal way of dealing with each other. Sometimes I cannot tell whether they are joking or being for real.

"Those are jobs for whores," Mfundo says and answers an imaginary phone.

"I want to go into movies," Mpumelelo says thoughtfully.

Mfundo breaks into a scornful laugh. I feel pity for Mpumelelo.

"You gonna finish the calendar now now. Clock thirty-one years," Mfundo says. "You must contact that father of yours in Joburg, ask him for something," he advises.

Nhlakanipho and Mpumelelo don't have the same father, but share a mother. Mpumelelo's father is a wealthy businessman empowered by BEE. For some years, he has featured on the list of South Africa's most influential people. Mpumelelo fell out with him when he was still in varsity and was staying at his father's place. Mpumelelo despises his father's taste for young women. He sleeps with women the same age as Nhlakanipho and I, Mpumelelo tells us.

"I don't need him," Mpumelelo says. "I just need my brother, Nhlakanipho, and my mother. In fact, I'm closer to you than to my father," Mpumelelo says, pointing at Mfundo.

"You cannot rely on me. I'm a hustler, a roller, I need money. You are a liability to me. I'm spending money when I'm with you," Mfundo shouts.

"I'm a liability to you?" Mpumelelo says, sounding surprised.

Remorse shows in Mfundo's face.

"My father is the richest man in Langa. Everyone knows him," Mfundo says. "He has never given me anything. He only took notice when people started speaking about me struggling. In that period, I only had two pairs of trousers. He called me again when they heard that I was part of a syndicate."

Mfundo pushes up the volume and dances. The night he stabbed his girlfriend started like this. Mfundo drinks from the bottle, draining off the remaining champagne, and stands next to a white cupboard in the kitchen.

"I'm rich, maaan . . . Mpumelelo," Mfundo says.

We are all gathered in the kitchen. Nthabiseng and the young prostitute are chatting in the lounge.

"So what, what do you want me to do?" Mpumelelo says.

"I'm rich, maaan." Mfundo sings a song about buying the block of flats.

The young prostitute's nose is red. She and Mfundo have been up all night. She is about to pass out on the couch.

"Hey, hey, hey!" Mfundo shouts, dragging her by the arm. He takes her to his bedroom.

After some murmurings outside the flat, Nthabiseng leaves Mpumelelo and goes home. Mpumelelo comes back inside. He is now kak drunk. He wants to take a plate from Mfundo's kitchen to his flat.

"Leave that plate," Mfundo warns.

"I'm taking it," Mpumelelo argues.

"What's wrong with you? You are not like this when your chick is not around," Mfundo says.

Mpumelelo walks from the kitchen with the plate. In a flash Mfundo takes out his gun and points it at Mpumelelo.

"You are not gonna come here and fucking disrespect me," Mfundo says, his eyes wild.

Nhlakanipho comes between them and pleads with Mfundo to put down the gun. Mpumelelo looks at Mfundo with careless eyes. Seeing Mfundo's dangerous expression, I push Mpumelelo out of the flat.

* * *

"I was only scaring him. I wasn't gonna do anything," Mfundo says, when the three of us are seated. "He's frustrated by that bitch of his. That's why he's acting up. She was all over me. I know bitches like that. Those are the sort of bitches we just fuck and slap, tell them to fuck off. Mangaliso probably has also fucked her. That's why Mpumi keeps saying Mangaliso is just a laaitie," Mfundo reasons.

I look the other way when Mfundo mentions my indiscretion.

"Mpumelelo has a jealous heart. He does not like seeing my riches. He does not realise, I worked hard to have all these things at such a young age," Mfundo says.

I don't see a difference between Mpumelelo and Nhlakanipho. They are both possessed by envy and are quick to shoot down people who are doing well.

"Mpumelelo is one of those that used Western medicines at initiation school. I know these things. I am a sangoma. There have been more times than I can count where I have dreamt of something and it happened in the exact way I dreamt of it," Mfundo says.

Though Mpumelelo has a degree in psychology, Mfundo is more perceptive.

Mfundo asks us to leave. "You boys must go home now. Don't compare yourselves to me. I don't have to wake up and report to a job," he says.

He walks us out of his flat. "You, Manga, you must stop fucking other niggers' women," Mfundo says, leaning against the front door. We all laugh at this.

* * *

I arranged to view a bachelor pad in Wynberg. I was soaked by a fierce rain as I left the station. I kept calling the owner, as I couldn't find the place. By the time I found the house I was so wet it was like I had taken a shower with my clothes on. The house was owned by a Muslim family. The wife took me to the back to show me the accommodation. It was an attractive space, with a kitchen and a bathroom. The rent was reasonable – two thousand eight hundred rand a month. I wanted to sign the lease there and then. But she said she still had to see other people. I knew she wasn't going to call me back.

My disappointment went on. Now I was looking for any place, regardless of how many people stayed there. Every place said more people were still coming and never got back to me.

* * *

Perhaps it's time I consider leasing a place of my own. The arrangement of renting a room from someone else can be suspect, as you are never certain of the actual amount that the place costs. I have seen a number of affordable two-bedroom apartments on the internet. One such place is in Kenilworth and goes for four thousand six hundred rand a month; I could split the rent with a flatmate. On contacting the agent for the flat, he says there's already someone interested who has first preference. He promises me that I'll have the second option.

The agent calls me after a few days; he says the place is now available. I arrange to view the apartment one afternoon after work. The flat is furnished. There's even a washing machine and a dryer. I really want to stay here. I agree to pay the deposit in a couple of days. I squeeze some money for the rent from my mother. Tongai is keen on moving in. He deposits his rent money into my account.

Chantel says "Good luck" as I carry my bags out of the flat. She's smoking a cigarette in the lounge. This comes as a shock. I only look at her and walk away.

Nhlakanipho and I help Tongai carry his belongings from his mother's flat in Newlands. Tongai also likes the new place. He calls it a window into a new life. We decide not to smoke inside our apartment. Nhlakanipho laughs about Tongai's room being much smaller than mine. Nhlakanipho does not seem happy about us finding this place; there's some sadness beneath his laughter.

We stay up till late on our first night in Kenilworth. Tongai is eager to get order and direction in his life. He suggests we pin up posters of writers for inspiration. Tongai used to stay with a bunch of musicians, including Kgotso. He says that those guys are disciplined and they have portraits of jazz legends in their rooms. I jokingly suggest that we invite people to open the house in prayer.

"That's a good idea," Tongai jumps up.

"No, I was only joking," I say.

*　　*　　*

Nhlakanipho pays us a visit the Friday after we move into the flat. He takes a bottle of Jack Daniel's out of his bag. I have some leftover skunk, which Nhlakanipho rolls. Tongai has filled the bookshelf in the lounge with his books. As drunkenness begins to weigh on us, Tongai shares his love for Dambudzo Marechera.

"He was the only person to heckle Mugabe, when Mugabe was giving a talk at Cambridge University," Tongai says. "I think Marechera was always fascinated by the relations between sex and violence."

From Marechera he goes on to JM Coetzee. "What makes him so great is the allegory," Tongai says. "In *Disgrace* it's no coincidence that he goes from Cape Town to Grahamstown. *Disgrace* was one of those rare, perfect books, in that everything was planned."

"That shit is dry. It reads like a textbook," I argue. "You know, I was in Gugulethu, at that hip-hop thing earlier in the year. There was this one lady emcee who owned the time. She took me to primitive Xhosa society; praise singers of old must have interacted with their communities in the way that she performed."

"A scholar will leave lasting works," Tongai hits back.

"Life is there and then in that moment. That lady touched me there and then, irrespective of whether she'll leave lasting works. Those lasting works will be like textbooks. Kids will be asking each other: 'How far are you with the book?' 'Eish, I'm only on chapter four.'"

"Coetzee knows language. He taught himself German," Tongai fires back.

"Good for him," I reply.

At moments like these, Nhlakanipho keeps quiet. He lights up when he speaks about businessmen. He follows the lives of

American tycoons. Whether we are interested or not, it does not seem to bother him.

*   *   *

We buy groceries together, Tongai and me. We fill the trolley with food we hope will last for the month. After work, we alternate on cooking supper. Tongai is a far better cook than me. He's even careful about the rice he uses. Before moving back to his mom's place, Tongai stayed in a commune in upper Newlands; the white landlady also lived with them. There, cooking was an effort, and they went to great lengths preparing meals. I often bumped into Tongai coming from Pick n Pay when it was his turn to cook.

Staying with a friend is easier; there's less bickering. Tongai is always reading. He takes a book with him to read on the train, every day on our way to work. I try keeping up with him. I read some of his books. One novel I go through is *Summertime* by JM Coetzee. It reads well right to the last page.

*   *   *

Preparing reports at work is no longer a challenge. Monday is my only busy day and I submit the findings on Tuesday. For the rest of the week I don't have anything to do. My manager has an air of pride. He communicates in a mechanical language using business terms that are common at the office – words like "liaise" and "strategise". Some of the workers do not like him. Behind his back they murmur about his snotty attitude. He refers to the older women by their first names, not saying "auntie" or "mama".

*   *   *

One evening Tongai was burning. "They have moved me in front of the shithole," he said, standing in front of the stove.

"Did they consult with you?" I asked.

"No, this morning they just told me to move to another cubicle. There's a new guy at the office," Tongai said. "It's that situation, the politics of space . . . you know, it's like in Constantia, the black workers come in the morning in a bus. And go home on the six o'clock bus. And that's their relationship with Constantia."

"Why don't you tell them you don't like the new space?" I asked.

"Imo take it like a nigger," Tongai said, wriggling his arms.

There's a submissive edge about the Zimbabwean guys I know. They appeal to the white structure so much and want the white life. In the process they sacrifice so much of themselves. Once we were preparing to go to a party. It was the birthday of a woman who had studied with Tongai. At Nhlakanipho's flat, Tongai was worried about the crinkled shirt I was wearing. They gave me a top to put on. Tongai even wanted to comb my hair.

In the night Tongai came to my room. He apologised for dumping his problems on me.

*   *   *

Tongai has lunch with his mother on Sunday afternoons. He says his mother loves him unconditionally. After heavy weekends of drinking he goes to the softness of his mother. I hardly ever talk with my mother. She calls me at times and we have mundane conversations. Tongai listens to a depressing radio programme on Sunday evenings called *This American Life*. It's about the blandness of lives led by Americans working dry jobs like call-centre agents.

*   *   *

Tongai has a strange habit of using my roll-on. Sometimes he asks for permission while in the act. He'll be standing in front of the mirror in my room, one arm raised, my deodorant under his armpit and ask "Do you mind if I use your roll-on?" if I walk into the room. This vexes me, as does his absent-mindedness. He often leaves his jeans in the lounge, and does not bother returning the ironing board to the wardrobe.

Tongai is doing his master's in African Studies part-time at UCT. For three years now, he has been wrestling with his thesis. This year he wants to submit it. In the past, his drinking got the better of him and he would end up losing focus.

Always one to have his ear out on the established arts scene, Tongai takes Nhlakanipho and me one evening to the Standard Bank National Youth Jazz Festival at the Baxter Theatre in Rondebosch. We enter the reddish facebrick complex through an electronic glass door. The wide staircase has polished brown railings. We walk down the carpeted aisles and are ushered to the last available seats. A representative from Standard Bank opens the evening with a speech. What sticks in my mind is his claim that you can gauge the civilisation of a people by their arts.

The performers take the stage, bowing to the audience. There is a cold splash of applause. Some of the guys we know from UCT do pieces. Kgotso does a trumpet solo. I know him from some parties and from around Observatory. The crowd seems to particularly enjoy Kgotso. The other performances revolt me. This is some Elizabethan crowd, sitting back asking to be entertained, and then applauding. Kgotso goes on to be the runner-up in the jazz category. He wins a prize of five thousand rand.

Outside, in the foyer, Kgotso is surrounded by his fellow musicians. He looks drunk and has a beer in his hand. With him is

Michelle, his girlfriend, who has curly ginger hair and a reddish complexion. Michelle had dated Tongai for a short while before moving on to Kgotso. Tongai was never able to consummate the relationship. He once spent an entire weekend with Michelle and was unable to get it up. Tongai goes over to hug Michelle and congratulates Kgotso, putting his hands together and almost curtseying.

I am steaming up. This gathering is getting up my nose.

"Fuck this shit," I whisper in Nhlakanipho's ear.

Nhlakanipho looks back at me.

"Fuck this shit, this whole gathering," I foam.

"What is wrong with you?" Nhlakanipho asks, looking at me.

"Fuck Standard Bank. Fuck this European crowd. Fuck this perception of art. Did you hear that speaker going on about art and civilisation?"

"Yeah, yeah, I also did not like that," Nhlakanipho agrees.

Tongai dances with the music crowd, lending his teeth for laughing. As the lights become dimmer, he bows out.

There are no taxis around to take us home. Rondebosch has quietened down without the sound of whistling taxi conductors. We have to walk back to Kenilworth. Tongai and Nhlakanipho do not seem to share my feelings about the concert. As much as I try to pass on my bitterness, they are not bothered. As consolation to myself, I decide never to attend such an event again.

*   *   *

Rasun understands my grievance. "That's some petty-bourgeois shit," he says about the music festival. Rasun says those are the sort of gigs his grandma goes to. We have drinks and play pool at Stones, a double-storey bar in Lower Main Road in Observatory.

A staircase leads into the bar. There are several pool tables inside with chairs against the wall. Rasun is always on the lookout for women we can score. We are rarely successful in this. Most nights he just drops me off at my place alone.

"So, you are staying with Tongai now," Rasun remarks. We are sitting at one of the tables on the balcony. From this position, Observatory lies below us.

I nod to Rasun's statement.

"He's a cool cat," I say.

Rasun scoffs. "You think so?"

"Yeah," I reply.

"He holds himself back. Beneath all that bowing shit, he has a lot of anger," Rasun says, ending with a thoughtful gaze at the street.

He has complained about Tongai in the past. Rasun feels that Tongai has good opinions about literature but will not write.

Tongai calls me to find out when I'm coming home.

"Is this cat checking up on you now?" Rasun asks after I end the call. "That is some bullshit. He doesn't care," Rasun says. "Come on, you gotta agree that is bullshit."

I laugh for the sake of being courteous.

"Does that cat cook for you?" Rasun asks.

I smile, look the other way.

Rasun cannot stand Nhlakanipho. He has told me that Nhlakanipho is a child, who thinks everything revolves around him. I agree; Nhlakanipho does have delusions of grandeur. In the past, Nhlakanipho has told me and Rasun that he wants to dent the universe.

Telling Rasun about Mfundo rouses Rasun.

"Cat, gangsters don't care about anyone but themselves," Rasun says. "I read about how they are initiated. They have to slaughter cats so that they learn to kill and not to care."

Just about all the tables on the balcony are occupied. The Stones crowd is mostly white, and so they play rock music. Rasun loves brandy and Coke. On some nights, we have up to six of these.

"Who the fuck does that?" Rasun cries out, when I tell him how Mfundo took Nhlakanipho and Mpumelelo to a brothel. "The gangster is gonna want a payback," Rasun warns. "I can already see him extorting money from Nhlakanipho."

"Nhlakanipho bought the cocaine and the booze the last time we chilled with the gangster," I tell Rasun. "Nhlakanipho even believes God brought this cat to us."

"Fuck . . . I think it might be too late for him. Nhlakanipho will be happy as long as he has some father figure patting him on the back. Something fucked-up happened with his father," Rasun says and looks at me with his small brown eyes. "You know all that shit he does, reading about famous businessmen and obsessing about rappers. He's looking for a father figure."

This sort of makes sense to me. There's always some famous man on Nhlakanipho's tongue. If it's not some rapper, then it's some tycoon. But the textbook view of people does not settle with me. People are more complex than that, and are just as able to analyse themselves.

"Cat, stay away from the gangster." This topic has really awakened Rasun. "It's like in *The Godfather*. They called this one lady to come take a photo with them. Then they said: 'You are now part of the family.' That's the shit; you cats are now part of the family."

"He did say that, we are now part of the family," I say.

"Fuck, you cats are in shit. Don't you dare mention my name to the gangster. If you do, I will know. You know what? I have magic," Rasun says, and places his right palm on the table. "Some fucked-up shit will happen to you if you mention my name to the gangster. I will kill you."

"You gonna kill me?" I say, smiling.

Rasun shakes his head at my disbelief, "Fucked-up shit will happen." Rasun does not doubt his claim.

"The gangster also has magic. He says he is a sangoma," I say.

"Fuck, I don't even want to meet this cat," Rasun says, looking terrified. He cannot let this talk of gangsterism go. He is not even paying any attention to women. Usually, he would have called me aside by now to tell me of some girl he had spotted.

"Cat, I don't think you understand. Every little thing matters to gangsters," Rasun says. "And they don't care about anyone else but themselves."

"He did say that to Nhlakanipho's brother. He said Mpumelelo is a liability to him: 'I'm a hustler, I need money,' he said."

"And what did Nhlakanipho's brother say?"

"He looked disappointed," I say.

"Then he's just as dumb as Nhlakanipho."

"That cat is on another tip. You know, I had to take him out of the flat; he was beefing with the gangster. He wanted to leave with a plate. The gangster was pissed off."

"The gangster is gonna bring that up again. Every little thing matters to them," Rasun says.

*   *   *

Rasun stops the car in front of my block of flats, allowing me to get off. On the way to my place he kept on threatening to kill me should I mention his name to Mfundo. I had to tell him to stop it.

Though I do not believe in magic, I am careful not to tell anyone what Rasun said to me. Subsequently, Rasun never mentions anything about having magic powers. Perhaps the liquor was to blame.

* * *

Tongai pelted through the door late one afternoon after work. He had a folded page in his left hand. I was sitting in the lounge.

"I was writing in the train, on my way from work," Tongai said, out of breath. "I have not written in such a long time," he said, unfolding the page. "Papa was never a preacher man," Tongai read in a manufactured voice, and then mumbled through an incomprehensible poem.

I told him I did not understand it.

"It's a poem about someone losing his mind," he explained.

It did not make any sense to me. It felt artificial, with no beauty, read in a mechanical tone.

"I'll have to go through it again, clean it up. I haven't done these things in a long time," Tongai said, like an expert in the field.

* * *

I found myself in the bottle store at the Pick n Pay in Claremont one Friday evening. I had been paid that day. I looked at the prices of liquor; the Veuve Clicquot champagne that Mfundo drank cost close to five hundred rand. I was not going to buy it. I settled for a straight of Jack Daniel's and two bottles of the cheaper J.C. Le Roux sparkling wine. I withdrew eight hundred rand from the ABSA ATM just outside Pick n Pay so I could buy two grams of cocaine. I had just over two thousand rand left in my account after paying my rent and my student loan.

I was in a carefree mood as I walked to Mfundo's place, amused at the irony of a brother like me holding all this expensive alcohol. I have never been one for prestigious drinks. When others were drinking Amstel, I'd have a Black Label quart because that sort of shit does not matter to me. The last time we were with Mfundo, he accused me of running from the guys when I have money.

Mfundo was with Mpumelelo in his flat. They both cracked up when they saw what I had in the plastic bag. Mfundo had on a white apron. He put the champagne in the deep freeze. He juggled steaming pots on the stove. Mfundo does things fast: he speaks fast, he walks fast.

"There should always be something green in a meal," Mfundo said, chopping green peppers.

He must have stabbed his girlfriend with a knife like the one he's using. I can imagine him chasing her around the flat.

Mfundo served us a fine meal of spicy pork sausages and mashed potatoes. Nhlakanipho and Zola, an accomplice of Mfundo's, had arrived in time for the food. Zola looked the part of a gangster in his black leather jacket. He drove a BMW Z4.

"Cocaine kills my appetite. It's better I eat first," Mfundo said.

Nhlakanipho finished first and went for a second helping, emptying the pots. I gave Mfundo money to buy us cocaine. He called the dealer. Mfundo often said that he bought from his own supply. I had never got coke on my own before. I didn't even have the numbers of any dealers. Whenever Nhlakanipho and I wanted some cocaine on our own, Mfundo had refused to give us the dealer's numbers. Mfundo often warned us about getting hooked on the drug.

Cocaine has never been sweeter than the stuff we had that night. My lips became rubbery. I spoke without any inhibitions, even beating on the carpet at times. I was running into a field of freedom, my lungs heaving in the open space. I saw everyone as a shadow bearing no threat.

Zola had messages to relay to Mfundo. They laughed about matters that I would have thought would make them nervous, some involving murder. Piecing this talk together, I was certain that it was about the war Mfundo had mentioned previously. From Zola it emerged that Mfundo was a wanted man. Zola joked that Mfundo should change the number plates on his car and that he should wear a balaclava when they went to Langa.

"They'll never get me," Mfundo asserted. "Since they missed me in Khayelitsha, they can forget about ever getting me."

"Hayi suka, people say you were so scared your gun was not even cocked," Zola teased.

"That was a blessing. I could have had four or five down. And ended up with those long cases that drag for three years."

Zola did not take cocaine. He was far more menacing than Mfundo. He barely said anything to us. Zola drank ciders.

"This thing can be resolved in one weekend . . ." Mfundo said. "These laaities don't realise that there are big dogs that can just say 'se gat' and end this whole thing." Mfundo threw his right hand in the air after saying this. "I don't want to lie, I am in hiding here. I have a lot more to lose than these laaities. How can I run around shooting it out with people who don't even lead the same lifestyle? They are not even on the same level mentally. I tell you what, those kids are going to end up killing each other," Mfundo said.

Mfundo and Zola reminisced about women. On some occasions they had slept with the same woman. According to Mfundo, his girlfriend still visited him. But her family did not want her to go to him, so she only came during the day. She had not fully recovered from the stabbing and had chest complications. Mfundo took out the sparkling wine from the deep freeze.

"That's them," Zola said after answering his phone.

Mfundo pulled out his gun from beneath the sofa cushions.

"Let me put something on," Mfundo said. He went to his bedroom, came back carrying a red panama. He and Zola left the flat and drove off in Zola's car.

I passed out on the sofa for perhaps an hour. When I looked up, Mfundo was pointing his gun at me. Nhlakanipho was fast asleep on the sofa next to me. Zola was standing beside Mfundo.

"Don't scare us, Mfundo," I said, even though I was not frightened.

"No, no, no, there are no bullets," Mfundo said, cocking the gun twice to show that there was indeed no ammunition. He took out the magazine and waved it in my face. Mfundo then threw the gun at me. I caught it out of instinct.

"Put it under the sofa," Mfundo commanded. "You must know where it stays. Maybe someday you'll have to use it."

I did as he said.

"Where were you guys?" I asked, still dazed from sleeping.

"Don't you know I'm also an assassin?" Mfundo said smiling. "But eish, I missed. I have to get another supply of bullets."

*　　*　　*

Drunkenness always makes me horny. I checked out a few spots in Claremont on my own, but I stood no chance of getting anything from these clean girls. I prefer easier girls who just grind on you. Some of the prostitutes in Kenilworth are attractive. I passed a younger one with full thighs on my way to my apartment. I thought of trying something with her but decided against it. I was so aroused I'd have to wank before going to bed. Sitting on the pavement in front of our block of flats was a woman wearing a bandana and a pink jacket.

"Don't you wanna come inside with me?" I asked her.

She looked up. "You gonna have to pay," she said in a coloured accent.

"How much?"

"One hundred and fifty."

"For the whole night?"

"I can stay for the whole night. But can you buy me KFC in the morning?"

"OK, I'll get you KFC."

I went to the Caltex garage to draw the money and also to get some condoms. She started undressing when we entered my bedroom. To get the first round out of the way, I tried fucking her between her breasts. It was awkward, my knees on her round belly, trying to get between her breasts.

"You know what? Just fuck me," she said, getting tired of the breast job.

"But the first round is short," I said.

"It doesn't matter."

She swallowed me between her thighs. Strangely, she was wet. She lay back as I fucked her. She was big. My hips were moving but I couldn't feel anything. She was also too quiet for my liking.

"Come on, act like you're enjoying it," I urged her.

She moaned softly and mechanically, and stopped when I ejaculated.

"Yoo, I'm so tired," she said, going to my wardrobe.

I had only one pillow. She took a jacket from the wardrobe and laid it on the bed as a pillow. Then she lay with her bandana on the jacket.

* * *

I still wanted to squeeze off some semen in the morning.

"You gonna have to make it fast," the woman said.

I had never had a blow job before. I shifted so that my erect penis was near her mouth.

"No, no, put on a condom," she said.

I rolled down a condom. Tongai walked into the room while she was sucking me on the condom. I felt his eyes from behind.

"Oh sorry, I didn't know you had company," Tongai said.

There's no way Tongai could not have known that I was with someone. Surely he would have heard our voices. It was a terrible blow job. I didn't feel anything. I had to masturbate for satisfaction. I gave the woman the money. It was my first time paying for sex.

"Don't you wanna get KFC?" I asked.

"No, I must go now."

* * *

We felt like the Obs vibe one Saturday evening. I boarded a taxi to Lower Main Observatory with Nhlakanipho and Tongai. We went to Café Ganesh, bought three quarts and took them upstairs to the balcony. Ganesh is cosy, with a few candlelit tables intimately close to each other. We liked sitting upstairs on the balcony as there were often people smoking weed who'd share with us. Tongai did not smoke spliff as it messed with his mind.

Holding cigarettes in our browny-yellow fingers, we bemoaned

117

our condition. Our lives have been about discontent, and Tongai was the most vocal about our looming failure. He made fun of the middle-aged men who frequented Ganesh; they had nothing, and we were in danger of ending up like them. Tongai dismissed our dreams of being writers.

"It's like Coetzee says: many will be called, though few will be chosen. For every successful poet, there are millions of failed poets," Tongai said. "I think what we fail to realise is that it is impossible to make a living as a poet. We need to get over these dreams of being celebrated. This is a working man's world. People progress at work, get promotions."

Nhlakanipho broke into a laugh. "I agree," he said.

"I think we'll never know unless we try. Being a writer, you don't need to carry it on your neck, letting it determine you socially," I said.

I spotted a woman I knew downstairs. She often sang and played guitar at open mic nights around Observatory.

"Do you know where we can get coke?" I asked her.

Her eyes vibrated with excitement.

"I can ask someone," she said.

She called a dealer. The cocaine went for three hundred rand, cheaper than what we were used to with Mfundo. I whispered to Nhlakanipho and we went out to withdraw cash. At the ATM, I closed my eyes and took the money. Nhlakanipho hadn't been paid yet. I also took the dealer's numbers from my guitar-playing friend. She came upstairs to where we were sitting and gave me the cocaine in a handshake. I felt a round piece of paper in my palm. Nhlakanipho ran the cocaine through a note like Mfundo did in the toilets at Ganesh. He tasted some of the white powder. It was neither as much nor as hard-hitting as Mfundo's cocaine.

We kept on going to the toilet without telling Tongai about the cocaine. Later, we hit some of the clubs in Observatory. These are dingy spots owned by Nigerians. The women here are more forthcoming. When I stayed in Obs I once took a woman from one of these spots back to my place. Even here there's a standard routine: buying the ladies drinks followed by raunchy dancing. The girls danced with their reflections in the mirror to the thumping music.

My mouth was sour from all the beer I had drunk. We walked to the Observatory station early in the morning after the clubs had closed. At this hour there were no security guards, so we could board a train without buying tickets. The cold sat on my skin. We tried to shake it off by smoking. Nothing fruitful ever comes from these nights.

*   *   *

I woke up sweaty, my chest and back wet. The sun outside the window was sad. I had violated my spirit. It was in tatters. This is not how I wanted to grow old. In an ocean of black shells, my feet were septic, becoming volcanic. This is not how I wanted to grow old. The prostitute had bent me inside out. This was not me. This black wind haunted me.

"I cannot go on like this," I said to Tongai. "I spent just about all my salary on drugs and alcohol."

"The thing is that these things will stop even being funny and just become sad," Tongai said. "I think it's a lack of self-esteem. We are scared of being with decent people. Even these places we drink in, there aren't any progressive people."

I listened to Tongai. Perhaps it was time to open up to his reasoning.

"This is not how I wanted to grow old. You know when I started these things, smoking and drinking, I didn't think I would be doing them for long."

Tongai said he had seen a psychologist during his third year at varsity. The psychologist said that Tongai was not one to drink in moderation. I too have not been able to limit my drinking. That afternoon we made a pact to stop drinking and smoking.

"You know, the happiest time for me was when I was doing form five in the old country," Tongai said. "I played first-team rugby, was a prefect. I did not drink for those eight months."

Tongai had been binge drinking since he was fourteen. His mother drank and often brought men into their house.

"That lady, where did you meet her?" Tongai asked.

"I met her in Kenilworth . . . asked her to come to my place."

"You mean you just met a lady and asked her to come home with you?" Tongai said disdainfully.

"She's actually a prostitute . . . I paid to sleep with her."

"I thought as much. I took a good look at her."

To survive until the next payday, we each contributed a thousand rand for groceries and I bought a monthly train ticket.

*　*　*

My life is a railway line along which the days drag, and I have become the rust-stained stones beside the line. I am tied to my job. The other workers know that there is not much for me to do. While they are busy the whole day, I listen to music. I have heard them mock my being a specialist. I carry last night's supper to work. I do not have money to buy myself lunch.

It is not proving difficult to stop smoking. I was already only smoking after work. I have never liked people to see me smoking. Even at university I had my cigarettes in isolation.

Tongai predicted that we would be more sensible without money. "It does not cost much to have coffee in a café, you know, and do the things that normal people do," he said.

I hear Tongai's voice in my sleep, chanting: "You will not go anywhere." I try opening the door to my room, but I cannot move it. I stagger like a drunken man and push on the window until the glass shatters. A fragment of glass pricking me on my mouth rouses me. I have just broken the window. I almost fall over. I have a cut beneath my left arm.

"What's going on here?" I hear a woman say.

It is early morning. She is standing below my window. Outside, the darkness is giving way to the first minutes of light. A gentle wind blows.

"I had a bad dream," I say.

"No one does that because of a bad dream. Those windows are shatterproof. They are not supposed to break," says a woman with dyed black hair. She is a member of the body corporate.

"You're gonna have to clean it up," she says.

I hurry to Tongai's room and switch on the lights. Tongai is lying on his back. I can tell that he is pretending to be asleep. There is fear in the way he is breathing. I tell him that I have just broken the window.

"You suffer from night terrors," Tongai diagnoses me. "You can go on the internet and research night terrors. One girl I stayed with also had them."

I take a black refuse bag from a cupboard in the kitchen and go around the parking lot picking up pieces of glass. I clear all that I can see, but with glass you are never certain you have got every piece.

"It is remarkable that you would fight like that," Tongai says later as we are getting ready to go to the train station. "I never imagined you as the violent type."

*   *   *

I read up on night terrors on the internet at work. This inspires me to write a poem I call "An Echo of Violence". I have been writing more poetry this year, though not as much as in my first year at university. I was depressed then and felt like an outcast. A terrible fear gripped me. I was afraid of people.

I send some poems I've edited to Ndlela and ask for his feedback. I decided a while back not to share my work with Nhlakanipho and Tongai. Nhlakanipho once accused me of writing for myself. Tongai wore a sedated smile as Nhlakanipho confronted me. Since then I have not shown them any of my writing.

I walk back to my apartment from Kenilworth station. All my work trousers are balloony around the waist. I tie them with a belt, but folds form in the thigh area. I feel awkward in my formal clothing. I bought all of it at Woolworths. I do not have any taste for the outfits. I wear the clothes as a soldier would put on his uniform.

I walk round the parking lot looking for pieces of broken glass I might have missed last night. Then I rest on the couch. This is where I'll have to sleep until the window in my room is replaced. Tongai wakes me. He offers words of encouragement: "It is only natural to want to sleep when you are under pressure, to want to escape and go to another place."

I'll have to fix the window when I next get paid. And that is a long time to sleep on the sofa.

*   *   *

The agent calls me on Friday at the office. "The maximum time a tenant can stay with a broken window is twenty-four hours," he says. The woman from the body corporate has told the agent what happened in the flat. I have to replace the window by today. I consider asking Ndlela for help. I decided a long time ago not to bother Nhlakanipho with my problems. He does not like to have his luxury infringed upon.

I call Ndlela and he makes an internet transfer into my account. The agent had given me numbers for window specialists in town. I call one glass store from outside the office during my lunch break. I do not want people at work to hear this conversation. They can fix my window by this afternoon. Even with the transfer from Ndlela, this will empty out all my money and Tongai agrees to lend me another hundred rand. I meet him in town. He withdraws the money from an ATM.

"At least you can tell people you once snorted cocaine and screwed a hooker," Tongai says as he hands me the cash. This comes as a shock to me, and I look at Tongai. He puts his hands together.

"I'm trying to cheer you up," he says and clears his throat.

The glass people call to say they are outside my apartment. My manager is not in his office. I inform another manager that I have to leave work early. I walk quickly to the station deck to get a taxi, as a train will take too long.

I find a blue van parked in front of our block of flats. I open the electric gate to allow the glass people access to the parking lot. They clean the window frame and put in the new glass. After they leave I feel depressed.

It is the start of the World Cup and my eyes are filled with tears. I sit on the couch, wrapped in my duvet, watching the

South African team marching onto the field. I jump up when we score the opening goal. Now it is tears of joy that fill my eyes. I am disappointed when the game ends in a draw.

*   *   *

Tongai surrendered during our second week of sobriety. He came back to the flat at six o'clock one Saturday morning. He got out of bed only at three the next afternoon. I know all too well how tiring alcohol can be. Tongai said he planned the drinking binge as he needed to release energy. I did not believe him. What makes things hard for Tongai is that they have a bar at work. Once he has had something to drink at work, he will continue into the morning.

*   *   *

So this is what Mfundo has been involved in. I find an open letter on the internet from a resident of Gugulethu, decrying gang activities in the township. The concerned community member says that the gang members don't live in Gugulethu, but rent flats in other parts of town. I am sure he is writing about Mfundo.

Nhlakanipho and Mpumelelo have spent far more time with Mfundo than I have. Nhlakanipho has even gone to upmarket restaurants with Mfundo and Zola. At least Mfundo does not know where I stay. I told Ndlela of my dealings with Mfundo and of taking cocaine on a weekend of drug bingeing. I felt I needed a sober person to talk to. Ndlela was shocked. He said I should guard against turning into someone I will hate.

Ndlela has not come back to me about the poems I sent him, though he did promise me a response.

*   *   *

Ndlela arrives unexpectedly in Cape Town. He calls me at work to inform me that he's in town. I am thrilled to hear from him. He has made arrangements to stay with his other friends.

I go to town that evening with Nhlakanipho and Tongai. The big-screen arenas are closed as they are already full. We decide to watch the Ghana–USA game at Neighbourhood in Long Street. Ghana is now the only African team left in the tournament. The streets are colourful, with people sporting soccer jerseys. There is barely any room to move inside the pub. Shoes step on shoes on the wooden floor.

Tongai is back in full swing, downing one beer after another. Ghana wins the game. We jump around and hug one another. But Nhlakanipho calls the Ghanaian team a bunch of amakwere-kwere.

"Hayi, you must see a doctor," Nhlakanipho says about my breaking a window in my room.

"I don't have money to see a doctor," I say.

"Can you imagine? Here's someone sick and he can't see a doctor because he does not have money," Tongai adds sarcastically. These guys flatten me, leaving me morose.

Nhlakanipho pushes his oversized belly like a trolley to the bar to buy drinks. He brings two beers for himself and Tongai. We sit on the crowded balcony. Though the night is screaming with excitement, it feels tired to me. Ndlela calls me, saying he is up the street at Capello. I walk over on my own to meet him.

Nhlakanipho does not want to come along. He says they won't allow him in, as he's not dressed formally enough. I am also wearing casual clothes. We all went to the same high school, Ndlela, Nhlakanipho and I, and we matriculated in the same year. I studied with Ndlela and we passed matric with distinction. Ndlela went on to do actuarial science at Wits. He always did better than me; when I got two As, he got five.

I'm surprised to see Ndlela holding an Amstel dumpy at Capello. *He drinks now.* He has long thick dreadlocks. He looks like one of those pictures you see in the careers pages of the newspaper of some dreadlocked guy standing next to a photocopier. I walk over to Ndlela. He is with some fast-looking brothers. They look like the sort who drive new cars and are into parties. Ndlela seems conscious of the beer he's holding. It dangles awkwardly between the first three fingers of his right hand. The people in here are stylish, the women made-up and in high heels. Ndlela moves to the beat of the music. He was part of a dance crew in high school. Back then, Ndlela and Nhlakanipho had dreams of being South African presidents. They were both vocal when it came to politics.

Ndlela wants to see his old comrade, Nhlakanipho. I am reluctant, but I agree to take him to Neighbourhood. Ndlela whispers to one of the guys he is with and we walk out of Capello.

"You don't see this in Joburg – white people walking in town at night," Ndlela says, as an old white couple strolls down the street.

* * *

Doris has joined Tongai and Nhlakanipho at a table on the balcony. Doris and Tongai have had an on-and-off fling for almost a year now. Tongai met Doris one Phuza Thursday at Pig and Swizzle and they slept together that same night.

Nhlakanipho laughs on seeing Ndlela standing next to me. He gets up, shakes Ndlela's hand, leans his right shoulder against Ndlela's shoulder and taps him on the arm before sitting down.

Ndlela does not drink again. He tries catching up with Nhlakanipho, who is acting strangely, laughing like a clown at things that are not so funny. Tongai extends his hand to Ndlela and then goes quiet. I sit on the side of the table facing Doris and Nhlakanipho. Doris seems agitated. She keeps looking over her shoulder and taking out her cellphone. Though Tongai has sex with this girl, he is horrifically ashamed of her. He often jokes about introducing her to his mother. Tongai does not want people to see him with Doris. She's not good-looking, and she smokes and drinks as much as he does. Tongai cites the smoking and drinking as the reasons for his embarassment.

"Can you take me to church on Sunday?" Ndlela asks me.

Nhlakanipho roars with laughter. "This guy does not go to church," he yells.

Tongai also has a good chuckle. He puts his hand on his mouth when I look at him.

"Manga is a Buddhist. Don't let these guys take you away from enlightenment," Nhlakanipho says.

"He dropped that. If you were a good friend you would have known that," Ndlela answers for me.

Ndlela knows of my troubles with Nhlakanipho. I have told him of Nhlakanipho's grating comments and the way he sees the negative in everything.

"We can remove a veil . . . hey, hey, hey," Nhlakanipho says, tapping me on my shoulder.

I hope he does not mention my episode with the prostitute.

It is getting late. Nhlakanipho and Tongai prevaricate about going home. I am tired and the company is also not kicking. Doris is not keen on leaving. She seems to still have some ideas for the night. She keeps playing with her cellphone. Ndlela takes the initiative, and decides that we should go to my apartment. We have to get Ndlela's bags from the other guy's car.

"Why are you friends with Nhlakanipho?" Ndlela asks as we leave the balcony.

I see Nhlakanipho out of the corner of my eye, listening, his right palm on the glass of the door.

"They are all I have," I reply.

*   *   *

Ndlela pays for the cab to Kenilworth.

"What did you do with your money?" he asks when I tell him I have no money to contribute to the cab fare.

"I spent it all on drugs and alcohol," I say brazenly.

We hop out of the cab into the cold and walk into my block. Ndlela sleeps next to me that night. We go way back, Ndlela and me. We experienced the pain of circumcision together. I have seen Ndlela's knees shaking as the traditional nurse dressed his wound.

The terror of the night comes back to me in my room. Ndela is fast asleep next to me. Something moves from my head to my chest. I get up, clutching the curtain. "Oh, God," I sigh when I come to my senses.

*   *   *

Ndlela suggested we go to the Waterfront on Saturday evening. He was in awe of the beauty of Cape Town in the cab on the way there. We watched one of the World Gup games outside on a big screen. On our way to get some burgers inside the mall, some white bird droppings fell on my left shoulder, leaving a mark on my jacket.

"Don't worry, it happens to us all the time," said a young woman standing with a friend next to an open bin.

I showed Ndlela the stain left by the bird poo.

"Why would it happen to you?" Ndlela said. "It means ululu-lwane – one who failed at initiation school and used Western medicines," he whispered.

I laughed.

I did use an ointment Ndlela's father brought to the initiation hut. I had developed a yellow line at the bottom of my penis. This worried the traditional nurse who was looking after us. We had to hide the ointment from men who visited us in the mountain. While we all used Zam-Buk at some point, Ndlela stayed clear of it. He graduated an untarnished man. I also first accepted Jesus at the initiation school. Ndlela's father, who was a pastor, prayed for me one night and I was born again. Ndlela's father said it took some convincing to get the white senior pastors in his church to endorse the circumcision. We went to the mountain under the guise that he was only doing the ritual so we could preach to the Xhosas, because if we were not circumcised they would surely not listen to us. I dropped my belief not long after returning to university. It was after getting circumcised that the night terrors began. I would wake up in an almost epileptic panic in the initiation hut.

*   *   *

I took Ndlela to Observatory for some variety. We went to Tagore's and had soft drinks upstairs. The carpet was almost pink.

"Now I understand why you became a drug addict," Ndlela ribbed me. "Everyone here is a druggie," he said, taking a look around the room.

There were pockets of people sitting on beanbags to our right.

Observatory is a bohemian suburb. You encounter a lot of self-proclaimed writers and poets here. This often goes with a certain look and a lot of pot. Tagore's is an intimate jazz bar. Everything is close together – the bar, the chairs and the stage area. There are photos on the walls of musicians performing, even one of Kgotso blowing his trumpet. An abstract painting hung above us.

"What we need now are people who can do the job. We need to buckle down and work. It's high time black students excel at university, come top of their class. And believe me, we are gonna run this economy," Ndlela said.

"What happened to your political ambitions?" I asked.

He shrugged. "I'm not political."

*   *   *

I hadn't been to church in Cape Town for more years than I could remember. We went to the His People ministry in Rondebosch. The service took place at the Baxter Theatre, near the UCT Lower Campus. The service was youth-flavoured, with spoken word and even some rappers. Ndlela sat in the row below mine. He was fidgeting with his BlackBerry. My phone vibrated in the left side pocket of my jeans. "The lady in the worship team," read a message from Ndlela. I smiled down at him, and he indicated the young woman with his head. She was light-skinned and petite.

As we were having coffee after the service, standing beside the dark-brown counter where refreshments were served, Ndlela spotted her chatting with some people. Ndlela pounced when she was on her own. Soon she was in stitches. Before being born-again, Ndlela had been known as an infamous womaniser at our sister school. He exchanged numbers with the woman and walked back to me.

"But she's too young," he said. "She's six years younger than me."

"Should you be looking for girls here?" I asked.

"If I don't look for them here, where else should I look for them?"

*   *   *

Tongai did not sleep at the flat on Friday or on Saturday. He did not bother telling me his whereabouts. Right after church, Ndlela wanted Nhlakanipho to join us at Mzoli's in Gugulethu. I sent Nhlakanipho a message telling him we were in a taxi on our way to Gugulethu, and then called him from Mzoli's. He was with Tongai. On the phone they sounded drunk.

"OK, we are coming," Nhlakanipho said.

The lines for buying meat at Mzoli's are mountainously long. The place peaks on Sundays. Expensive cars are parked in front of the chisa nyama, on the street running parallel to Mzoli's. It gets really busy, with people popping in and out of cars. I do not like the gluttony of people carrying around buckets of meat and alcohol. Ndlela was standing beside me. He had packed his bags in the morning and taken them to church. We sat in the tavern after ordering the meat. You place your order at the butchery and they braai the meat for you. The tavern was crammed. House music was blasting from the speakers.

"Do you think you are anywhere near your potential?" asked Ndlela.

"I don't even know what potential I have any more," I said, after a moment of thought.

Ndlela nodded. "You are one of the exceptional talents," he said.

I blushed.

"The race is not always for the swiftest," I replied. "I know of guys who took longer than me to graduate who are now doing well. Perhaps they were better able to play the game. I have never been able to sell myself."

"At some point you gonna have to stop putting yourself down," Ndlela said.

Nhlakanipho called, and asked me to place an order for meat for them.

"We have already bought, I can't do that," I said.

"Hayi, you guys are selfish, you and Ndlela," Nhlakanipho said and dropped the call.

I told Ndlela of Nhlakanipho's gripe. I suggested we queue again to place an order for him. We went to the butchery. After a few minutes standing in the line, Nhlakanipho called and said they were not coming.

"He didn't want to come," Ndlela said. "He has avoided me the whole weekend. He is probably afraid that I will outclass him."

Ndlela's flight was at half past three. He had to be at the airport by three. From Gugulethu there is no direct transport to the airport, so we waited on the side of the road opposite Mzoli's for an iphela, those run-down cars that take people round the township. We were hoping we could convince a driver to take us to the airport.

"We should be seeing practical progress now," Ndlela said. "There does not need to be any grand ideas. There's no reason for you not to have a small car, or to be able to save a bit each month. You see those kids I was with at Capello? They also did accounting at UCT. They stay in nice apartments and drive decent cars."

I hold Ndlela in high esteem. When he speaks, I listen. He

raised me up in high school. Before he came to our school in grade ten, my marks were falling. His friendship encouraged me.

"One of the things I like about the church is the theme of redemption and brotherhood. At church we look out for each other; we help when one of us needs a job. It's a pity you can't believe in this God who turned Himself into a mini-Him and died on a cross."

I wanted to laugh at this. Two drivers we stopped said they would not be able to take us to the airport. We were running out of time. Earlier at the tavern I had spotted a brother I stayed with at res back at varsity. I was his senior. I went back to the tavern searching for him. He agreed to take us to the airport. This guy was from Langa. He complained about the gang war, saying he does not drink in Langa any more.

* * *

Back at the flat, Tongai is pale. He, Doris and Nhlakanipho have been drinking for the past two days. He takes over a meal I am preparing and burns the chicken. The grease and chicken skin are left stuck in the pot.

"I'm sorry," Tongai apologises.

"It's fine . . . Don't worry about it," I say.

I settle for a tuna sandwich for lunch. Tongai got me into tuna. Whenever we buy groceries, Tongai makes it a point to get tins of tuna. As we eat in the lounge, he goes into an obscure recollection of a past relationship. "That bitch was in her mid-thirties," Tongai remembers. He does not usually use vulgar language.

"She had another lover. We would just fuck," he says.

My mind closes up. Tongai goes on rambling. He curses out of the side of his mouth. This anecdote is too weird. I excuse myself and go to my bedroom. I had been planning on writing. I have already written notes on a theme I want to touch on, when the world around me was humming a tune about what success is. I get lost in the many corners of the concept. I just start typing on my computer, not knowing where the story is going. The opening scene blossoms in front of me. Excited, I run to the kitchen to make myself a cup of coffee.

This is beautiful, I think, while reading over my words. I have to be gentle with this. Tongai enters my room. He finds me sitting in front of the computer. Tongai wriggles his upper body, spits insults about the woman he was speaking of earlier.

"Hey, you are cursing like a sailor today," I remark.

"Hayi, the anger of the repressed," Tongai says and goes out the door.

* * *

In the morning I see Tongai's shadow passing my room. He is running to the lounge. He goes back to his room panting, holding his Bible.

* * *

My manager had previously said something about me running time and motion studies. Now he wanted me to go ahead with the project. I would have to time employees doing their work and infer what their productivity ought to be in a typical working day. I was not looking forward to the assignment. It made people out to be like cows. My manager gave me a deadline for submission. I made arrangements with people to monitor them doing their work. In all the offices I visited, the attitude was resistant. I pushed through and gathered the data. The numbers were ridiculous. Some of the estimates I came up with meant productivity would have to increase by as much as five times. I stalled in giving my suggestions to my manager. I knew his memory was not sharp. He called me to his office when he realised that the project was late.

"The numbers are not adding up," I explained to him.

"But you had a deadline."

He had a pink patch on his lower lip – from drinking, I guessed.

I sent him what I had come up with. There was a furore in the office. This graduate is full of kak. It was decided to increase the level of productivity in increments.

I had stopped applying for jobs. I submitted my CV for so many positions, but no one was coming back to me. Ndlela had sent me information on some job openings. I contacted these people, sent them my documents. Some asked for my academic transcript. None of them called me up for an interview. I lost all hope of settling another job. My contract at Trilce would expire at the end of the year. I doubted they'd make me an offer. I also did not want to stay. Trilce Health is just an administration company. There would never be any high-level tasks. They took in graduates because it looked good to the government to say they were contributing to nation-building.

*   *   *

Weed is not as corrupting as alcohol, so I still smoke the herb every now and then. The only problem is that once I blaze zol, I crave a cigarette. I bite my tongue and ignore the craving. One Friday at Nhlakanipho's place, I smoke some zol while he smokes the spliff and drinks alcohol. Later, we link up with Tongai at Babbo Fusioné Lounge in Claremont. The night is soft.

Bright, scantily dressed students usually fill the place. We find Tongai sitting at a table a couple of metres from the bar. Babbo is rather small. There's a 72 cm screen above the bar area that shows music videos. Tongai notices that I have had something to smoke.

There is a group of meaty women on the dance floor. One couple have simulated sex. They pull a short man from his table to join them. He jives between them. He has an animated way of dancing, swiping at invisible flies. He comes over to our table afterward. He has a peculiar British accent. I don't know whether he's putting it on.

"You guys want pussy, right?" he says.

Nhlakanipho nods and laughs.

He looks at me. "You want pussy, right?"

"No, not really . . . I just came here to have a good time," is my response.

He looks me in the eye. "Do you go to church?" he asks.

I shake my head. "No," I smile.

"Does this guy go to church?" he asks, staring at Tongai and Nhlakanipho. "Jeez, you are very good, guy."

His dark eyes peer through me. It's as if he's stealing bits of my soul.

"Do you want money or humanity, and at what cost?" he asks after a silent moment looking through the holes in my face. "If you are something I am nothing, and if I am something you are nothing." Then he goes back to the girls.

One of the women this brother was dancing with leaps onto our table and moons Nhlakanipho and me. She is wearing black tights and a frilly white top. Her head is close to her knees as her buttocks go up and down. Nhlakanipho is impressed, and he giggles like a child. The women leave with the brother with the British accent. They drive off in a white BMW.

* * *

The guy with the accent made an impression on me. I go over his words in my bedroom. I write about the incident in my notebook. In my desire to be a writer I have not made any sacrifices. In his discreet way, Tongai once said that the musicians he stayed with do not have a Plan B; they are not your bankers-slash-poets.

* * *

What really made me resign from Trilce was when a team leader was appointed and I was moved from my cubicle. Without bothering to clear things with me, the manager, wearing a smile, ordered me to move to another section. I arranged to see the graduate programme coordinator later that week. I told him I wanted to resign. He started telling me how well the other graduates were doing, how some had been offered permanent positions. Without showing any disappointment, I said I was happy for them. His tactics did not bother me. I had to serve a month's notice before becoming free. It's crappy how they owned my time. Even if I did not have any work to do, I had to show up at the office.

* * *

Tongai asks me to vacate the apartment between six and seven one evening, as he has a session with a life coach. He says this is a woman from Zimbabwe whom his mother organised. I sense water rising up the walls in the flat. I have a bad feeling about this. Tongai cleans the flat in the late afternoon in preparation for the visit. He sweeps the carpet in the lounge, walking barefoot. He then takes a shower with cold water. We would normally switch off the geyser before going to work and put it on again in the evening before sleeping.

"No one likes an unsuccessful person, not even the unsuccessful," Tongai chants in the shower.

I told him that.

I decide to go for a jog during the time Tongai wants me out the flat. He is still barefoot, though he has now dressed up. On my way out of the flat I see a dreadlocked woman walking barefoot in the corridor. I know that this is the life coach. I direct her to our flat. Her eyes are teary; she looks like someone who has just come from a forest.

*   *   *

Tongai is still with the life coach when I return from my run. They are sitting at the table in the lounge. I look the woman in the eye, shake her hand and introduce myself. Never have I been this afraid of looking at a woman. Oil settles in my spirit. I do not like her. And there is no way for me to ask Tongai not to bring her to the apartment again.

"Thank you for being such a good sport," Tongai says softly, his hands together, after the life coach has left.

*   *   *

I ask Tongai about the life coach after a few days.

"I wish I could see her more often," he says. "I don't know if you ever read them, but she left some notes on the table."

"No," I say, shaking my head.

"They're there on the table," Tongai says in surprise, pointing.

I had noticed the many pieces of paper on the table. *But why would Tongai expect me to read his private documents?*

* * *

Tongai and Nhlakanipho still drink together on the weekends. I try keeping my interaction with Nhlakanipho to a minimum. He leaves me with a bitter taste. Nhlakanipho wants to control, wants people to listen to him. And the things he says about others are negative. He disparages everyone around him, even his own brother.

Tongai came to my room in the dark. It was two in the morning. He showed me a message from Nhlakanipho on his cellphone. Mpumelelo and Nhlakanipho wanted a place to sleep. Mfundo was threatening to kill them. I told Tongai it was fine for them to come over.

We waited in the lounge. Tongai went downstairs to open for them. Mfundo's girlfriend was also with them. Mpumelelo was wearing his grey coat. They filled the couches in the lounge. I did not know Mfundo's girlfriend, Nokuzola, was this beautiful. She told us that Mfundo had taken everyone out to Cubaña. The guys went to the toilet to snort cocaine. Mpumelelo, worried that Nokuzola was on her own, left the guys and returned to the table. When Mfundo came out, he found Nokuzola and Mpumelelo laughing.

"No one laughs with my girlfriend," Mfundo said.

They thought he was playing.

Mfundo's face hardened. He grabbed a glass from the table and smashed Mpumelelo behind the head.

"Why did you do that?" Mpumelelo cried out.

"It's not the first time you are disrespecting me," Mfundo said.

Nokuzola ran out with Nhlakanipho and Mpumelelo. They took Mpumelelo to hospital. He was given three stitches.

Since then, Mfundo has been threatening over the phone to take them out. I wondered to myself why Mpumelelo did not ask Nthabiseng for a place to sleep.

I got weed from my room. Mpumelelo looked relieved when I gave him the grass. He rolled with telephone book paper. I did not have any Rizlas.

Nokuzola shook her head when I offered to pass her the joint.

"So Mfundo was in the wrong, but we have to be the ones that run because he is a gangster," I said, trying to make sense of things.

"I don't know where you guys get this idea that Mfundo is a hardcore gangster. Mfundo is not a gangster. If he was a real gangster, why is he running from the boys from Gugulethu?" Nokuzola said.

Strangely, I did not see any evidence of a scar on Mpumelelo's head. I stole glances at him. His eyes were red.

"Mfundo and his friends slept with those boys' girlfriends. That's how this whole thing started," Nokuzola informed us. "Those boys are seventeen and eighteen years old. They do not wear fancy pointed shoes like Mfundo. They wear Chuck Taylors and shoot like idiots. Mfundo was almost killed in Khayelitsha; a bullet grazed his chest," she said.

Nokuzola's lower lip was longer than her upper lip. She was wearing a black beanie. There was something alluring about her. I wished I could hold her.

"I find myself asking, whatever happened to normal things?" Tongai burst out. "Whatever happened to going to movies? What sort of life are we leading, where we have to be running from the likes of Mfundo? Why are we even associating with such people?"

We laughed at Tongai. He gets like this sometimes, bringing out things his grandmother told him.

"Mfundo only got himself a gun now that this thing started. The other one, Zola, he does not even carry a knife. He's a tenders boy. In East London, Zola does not want to be seen with Mfundo; he does not want his business partners seeing him with people who are into credit card scams. It's that cocaine that makes Mfundo act like some fierce criminal. When he's had that thing, he starts with all this nonsense of being a gangster. Mfundo is actually sweet, but he wants people to think he's some hairy monster," Nokuzola said.

Nokuzola's right palm was on her forehead. Her fingers were trembling.

"He's hurting the people that care for him. And doing nothing to those kids that want to kill him," Nokuzola reflected.

There was trouble in Mfundo's home. Mfundo's father beat up the mother and Mfundo wanted vengeance on his father. Nokuzola had to mediate. She does not know why she came back to Mfundo after the stabbing. Mfundo has a pending case for attempted murder. There is nothing that Nokuzola can do to have the charges dropped; the case is now in the state's hands.

* * *

One thing Tongai does is book reviews. These are published in the *Cape Times*. He keeps clips of the newspapers with his reviews. He has shown me some of them. They are written in an academic tone with dry humour.

One Saturday afternoon, Tongai wraps a white scarf around

his neck. He carries a white sling bag on his shoulder. This arty look doesn't suit such a tall and well-built guy; it suits slender women. I liked those sorts of chicks at some point in my life. I thought they had something to say. I was being silly; dressing in a certain way does not mean anything. They try too hard to be different, to look the part of artists. I have seen them in taxis with obscure haircuts. It is all too much effort. It is a burden on them.

It is the weekend of the Cape Town Book Fair at the convention centre in town. Nhlakanipho and I tag along with Tongai. There is a beggar in front of the entrance to the station. His pale legs are exposed under his short blanket. His body shakes as he wheezes. Nhlakanipho stands still, shakes his head. "This is sad," he says and walks away.

We continue on to the convention centre. There are shining stools in front of the orange structure. Lines of trees colour the otherwise grey atmosphere. It is the middle of winter. It is busy inside the convention centre. I spot a famous actress coming down the stairs.

* * *

The expensive food at the book fair irritates me. You have to pay close to twenty rand for a cup of coffee. There's no way I'm buying anything here. Nhlakanipho gets himself a sandwich. I sit at a table with him. Tongai hurries inside the main hall to attend some of the seminars. Nhlakanipho and I look at the programme and opt to wait outside.

"Something happened this morning," Nhlakanipho says. "Mpumelelo and Nthabi were fighting outside the flat. Some of the tenants called the police. Luckily no one got arrested. Mpumelelo hurt his hand in the fight."

All this Nhlakanipho says softly, not looking at me.

"That's why I'm surprised that they are going ahead with the birthday party tonight."

I nod quietly. We have been invited to Nthabiseng's party at the Spur in Newlands.

*   *   *

Tongai returns after a couple of hours. We do not ask him exactly what sessions he went to. Tongai is excited. He plans to attend Achille Mbembe's talk in the morning. I find Tongai's fascination with African intellectuals pathetic. These guys keep coming up with verbose theories, whereas circumstances are not changing.

We cruise back to the taxi rank. In the taxi, Tongai is on a high.

"I had forgotten how good it feels to attend such events. Imagine now if I were to be seen with Doris in such a place," Tongai says, putting on a mocking face.

"I don't understand what your problem is with this girl. She's good enough for you to sleep with her. Why are you so ashamed of her? Is it something systematic, establishment?" I ask.

"It's not that . . . it's just hatred," Tongai says. "No, no, that did not come out properly. It's just . . ."

"It's like you going to Trilce with that prostitute," Nhlakanipho pierces me.

This puts me off everything. *Why does Nhlakanipho have to use that against me?* When we argue it is never about principles but rather a clash of egos. He strives to win debates to satisfy his ego.

*   *   *

Mpumelelo is sitting alone in the Spur with a beer. The restaurant is located upstairs on a corner in Newlands, on Main Road. Just down the road is Westerford High School. Tongai's mother stays in a block of flats nearby. This is a transitory place, taking in taxis in motion and people doing their shopping. Nthabiseng is still doing her hair at a friend's place. Tongai, Nhlakanipho and I sit down at the same table as Mpumelelo. I call a waitress over to ask the prices of soft drinks.

"There's a certain way of asking that," Mpumelelo says after the waitress has left, raising his hand.

Mpumelelo and Nhlakanipho look at each other. I'm starting to hate every minute of this. I plan to leave as soon as Nthabiseng arrives. Tongai also wants to go home. "Just make sure you pay your part of the bill before you leave," Nhlakanipho says.

Nthabiseng waltzes in wearing a pink dress. She has applied make-up, which hides the blemishes on her face. She is with two of her friends. They sit at a table to our left.

After finishing my drink, I ask, "How does it work with the bill?" I want to settle my amount and leave with Tongai.

Nhlakanipho and Mpumelelo do not answer my question. Tongai takes the burden of announcing our departure on himself. He goes to the ladies' table, wishes Nthabiseng a happy birthday, bows and excuses us.

"You guys haven't even eaten," Nthabiseng says, looking worried.

"OK, we'll stay for the food," I say to allay Nthabiseng's concern.

I stay on only to keep the peace. Nhlakanipho announces that he has stopped drinking and smoking. He has been clean for four days. Tongai excuses his drinking on this occasion.

"You are only fooling yourself," Nhlakanipho says and looks at me.

"Manga did his thing without any grand announcements. You have done very well," Tongai says.

When the food arrives, it is a feast. There are ribs, seafood, chicken wings, all on a huge platter.

Mpumelelo wanted to invite some of his homeboys. But Nthabiseng only wanted Tongai and me at her party.

"This is way too much for four people," Mpumelelo says.

"I told Nthabiseng that she does not have any friends." Mpumelelo says this loud enough for Nthabiseng to hear.

We dig into the meat.

"It's not every day that one gets to eat like this," Tongai says.

"And this is coming from people who wanted to leave," Mpumelelo scoffs.

This makes me regret staying.

Nhlakanipho starts with a cigarette and ends with a beer. He even drinks some of Mpumelelo's brandy.

I watch the proceedings, my arms folded. I do not have the presence of mind to take part in the conversation. Mpumelelo's tongue is loosening and becoming slippery. Surrounded by a mound of food, Nhlakanipho shares the story of a street kid he saw in town. *That's the problem with people. Everything becomes a front. It looks cool to care about the homeless at the dinner table.*

Mpumelelo leaves for close to ten minutes. He comes back wearing his grey coat. *He must have gone to his apartment to get it.*

"Nthabiseng loves you, Mangaliso. Believe me when I say so," Mpumelelo says.

Nthabiseng's friends look in our direction from their table. It is bizarre. We are two separate entities at the same party. We have not spoken to them.

"Hey," someone shouts.

Waiters walk down the aisle. They put on an uninspired show for Nthabiseng, who blushes as they sing the birthday song. We all clap after the performance.

I have been silent and my mouth is becoming sour. Nhlakanipho keeps bringing up sophisticated pieces of information, quoting authors from book launches we have attended. The funny thing is that he professed to being bored at these events. I'm tired of listening to him. He pushes on, shoving his words down our throats. No one really interacts with him; it's a one-man show.

"Mangaliso looks like he is sitting in a boardroom. Come on, loosen up," Nthabiseng says from her table.

I scratch the back of my head.

"This guy does not even attend board meetings at Trilce; he takes the minutes," Mpumelelo barks, scratching his throat.

I put on an exaggerated laugh. "That's a good one, hey," I say.

Tongai continues eating as if nothing is happening. I marvel at him. He is the sort of person who would put up with all kinds of shit from people and still eat the food they give him. He has lived and lost all sense of pride.

I understand Nhlakanipho tonight. From the beginning, his life has been about gaining social acceptance. His parents sent him to Model C schools for high school. But his township origins cause him to second-guess himself constantly. At times he is quick to say other people think they are better than him. The flag of having gone to Model C schools fits well in the township streets, where he becomes better than others. He probably gets the gossiping from home. His family must be busybodies, into everyone's business.

Nhlakanipho seems to be enjoying the cruelty that his brother has been meting out to me. He calls out to Mpumelelo and rubs his shoulder. I thought that Nhlakanipho would stand up for me. Heat rises from my fingertips and burns in my chest. I look at the knife next to me. I could stick it in Mpumelelo's neck. I seriously consider smacking him with a glass. I wouldn't mind taking on both of them. I don't know what they really did to Mfundo. Maybe they also disrespected Mfundo like they are doing to me. Maybe Mfundo did not put up with their bullshit.

"Fuck this shit," I curse under my breath.

I get up from the table and leave. I switch off my phone outside the restaurant. The walk back home cools me.

* * *

Nhlakanipho sent me an e-mail at work suggesting that we see a play. I played along, though I was fully aware that he was testing the waters, and that he would surely inform Mpumelelo of my response. I agreed to book us tickets on the internet. It turned out that the show was fully booked. "It's fine, I just thought it would be something nice to see," Nhlakanipho said.

I had been bumping into Bridgette at the taxi rank in town on my way home from work. I used to admire her from afar on campus. She smoked, wore spectacular sunglasses, and part of her G-string showed beneath whatever fabric covered her legs. I took my chances at the taxi rank and asked for her number. She gave it to me without any hassles.

* * *

The sun is setting one Friday when Nhlakanipho knocks at my door. He is wearing my T-shirt. I left some of my stuff at Nhlakanipho's apartment when I moved from Vredehoek to Kenilworth.

"You'll have to excuse me," Nhlakanipho says, with his hands together like Tongai. "I couldn't resist this T-shirt."

This pricks me. But I let it slide.

I have just discovered Gil Scott-Heron. Every day, I listen to his music. I haven't been this excited about music in a long time. It is pleasant to the ears and yet he was also saying something. I share my newly found treasure with Nhlakanipho. I sing along to the sounds playing from my computer. I tell Nhlakanipho all I know about Gil Scott-Heron, his struggle with drugs, and his time in prison.

After listening for a few minutes, Nhlakanipho dismisses the exercise. "Hayi suka, this guy is a druggie," he says.

What was I expecting? I had forgotten that Nhlakanipho never has anything good to say about anyone. I feel ashes in my soul while chatting with Nhlakanipho. He goes on a rampage, crushing Mpumelelo. I dread listening to the cold air coming from his mouth. He is violently bitter.

"Let's get some snow . . . I still like snow," he suggests.

"No, I can't . . . not now."

"Why not?" he asks.

I do not answer his question. I leave to pick up Bridgette and her friend at the Caltex garage. We buy two bottles of wine at 7-Eleven. Nhlakanipho also knows Bridgette, and they get chatting back at the apartment. Nhlakanipho uses some of the phrases in my writing when he speaks. He does this with a careful air, drawing attention to the words. I note this. I don't know how he would know them.

Bridgette still smokes as much as she used to in varsity. I lay down the ground rule that they cannot smoke inside the flat. Nhlakanipho resists. He first lights his cigarette in the house before going outside. He always has to find a way to undermine me.

Bridgette does not look so fine any more. Her lower lip is almost navy from smoking. Her behind is nicely cupped in the black tights she's wearing. Bridgette shares a flat in Century City with TK, her friend. TK is reserved. She says she does not drink wine. She is chubby, her whole body is full. I relate to TK, as she's also lost her job. The management at her previous workplace picked up on her absenteeism. She would go for as long as a month without going to work. A doctor friend of hers would write her medical notes.

TK urges the others to finish their wine. We then walk to Hobnobs in lower Kenilworth. Hobnobs is located below the railway station. This neighbourhood has a gentle air, with coffee shops and a few pubs. Hobnobs consists of an outside area with several benches and a bar inside with a couple of pool tables and gambling machines. After two vodka and limes, TK relaxes. She has a spirited attitude. Before returning to South Africa with her parents, she spent her high school years in America. There she says she was part of a sorority. When I probe her, she does not divulge what the sorority was about.

Tongai joins us later in the evening, and he and Nhlakanipho drink quarts of beer. Tongai is very polite.

"Hayi, you guys are terrible writers," Nhlakanipho bursts out.

"Who . . . me?" I ask, my hands pointing at my chest.

"How can you write when you are not happy? Fuck Steve Biko, fuck Frantz Fanon."

"Easy, man, you have not even read anything by Frantz Fanon," Tongai says.

"I don't have to. I know what he's about. How can you write

anything when you are not free? Do you know where the best writers are? Oh, you guys won't believe it . . . they are in India," Nhlakanipho says.

I guess Nhlakanipho gets his faith in the Indians from yoga. He often tells us that he meditates at his house. He must believe that yoga is a liberation that the Africans do not have.

*   *   *

Bridgette sits on my lap. We have left the others to sit at a table in the corner. I watch her from behind as she goes to the bathroom.

"Shit, I'm drunk," Bridgette whispers on her return. "I just puked in the toilet," she says. Her eyes are unsteady.

This is such a turn-off. I lose all desire to kiss her. Bridgette's conversation becomes confusing. She loses me when she speaks about being scared of trees. She fears that old trees watch her. When walking at night she worries that the trees could speak to her.

*   *   *

On our way back to the apartment, Nhlakanipho lies on his back on the pavement listening to music on his cellphone headset. He kicks his legs on the ground. We all stop to watch him. He becomes animated, holding his arms tight at his sides and stamping on the grass. He makes all of us listen to the song after he gets up.

In front of our block of flats, he tries persuading the ladies to go somewhere else with him and carry on drinking. TK says she is tired. He eventually gives up after much pleading. In the early hours of the morning, TK grills some chicken in the oven. We read to each other from some of Tongai's books in the lounge. TK brings the meat to us, dripping in a creamy sauce. TK is one fine cook.

With no intention of doing anything with Bridgette, I get them a duvet. TK and Bridgette sleep on the couch.

* * *

Later on Saturday afternoon we keep TK and Bridgette company while they wait for a taxi in Main Road. I see Nhlakanipho passing his business card to Bridgette. He has a smug look on his face afterwards. I have come to realise that Nhlakanipho is steaming with hatred, as he is always gossiping about people. A man like that is dangerous.

"It was nice having you guys around," I say and hug TK as a taxi waits for them. Nhlakanipho also embraces TK and says he hopes to see them soon.

At night I dream I am pushing Nhlakanipho in the corridor, yelling "in the name of Jesus". I wake up standing by the window. *Nhlakanipho is a poison that I do not need now that I am writing. Such negativity could ruin my flow.* I believe in dreams. A few times I have dreamt of people I haven't seen in a long while. And the next day the person will call me. Nhlakanipho has torn me too many times. In my body the waters are rising. He has been abusing me since varsity. Our friendship is a falsehood. He even influences how others perceive me. Both Mpumelelo and Nhlakanipho are presences I do not need. No one wishes anyone well. And it's not like I am compelled to interact with them.

* * *

"Man, I think I have had enough of Nhlakanipho," I say to Tongai in the morning.

"I noticed yesterday you were in a foul mood. What was the matter?"

151

"I realised that this guy is full of hate."

Tongai turns around. "Hey, Mangaliso," he sighs, "both those guys, Nhlakanipho and Mpumelelo, they are vindictive gossips. Haven't you noticed that they never have anything good to say about anyone? You are not the first person that has warned me about Nhlakanipho. Some of my friends have told me: 'Hayi, that comrade is not good.' I even have an e-mail from one friend of mine who told me to stay away from Nhlakanipho," Tongai confides.

I did not want Tongai to take sides. I was doing this for my own peace of mind.

"Ey bra, I don't want you to take decisions on my account. You should make up your own mind."

"Even Mom has warned me about Nhlakanipho," Tongai says.

"I think now that people are growing older, they are just be-coming unpleasant personalities," I reflect.

"Maybe this is something we have to talk about, the three of us," Tongai suggests.

"There's nothing to talk about. I have had enough of Nhlakani-pho."

I call Nhlakanipho. His phone goes to voice mail. I feel relieved, as speaking to him would have been difficult. I send him a mes-sage: "I have had enough of your negativity. Please keep your dis-tance from me. Let's not even pretend we are friends."

When he does respond, Nhlakanipho writes: "Very well then."

* * *

"So you finally agree that Nhlakanipho is full of shit," Rasun said.

I nodded.

Nhlakanipho had been a lemon tree in my life for a long time. I was glad he was no longer around to torment me. Rasun had spun a five-rand coin and decided we should go to Stones in Observatory. It had been two weeks since I severed my friendship with Nhlakanipho. Rasun and I were both not working. He had never been keen on the idea of a job. Since graduating with a degree in film, he had stayed at home for close to two years. He was trying to make a film based on a novel he liked, but it wasn't taking off.

I did not show up at the office on my last day of work. They had planned a farewell for me. I did not want to go through with the charade.

Rasun vanished into his thoughts. He was spinning the five-rand coin and nodding to himself. We laughed a lot. He is care-free and I like that. Nowadays my chest is bubbling with joyful freedom. Each morning I work on my story. Then I walk the streets, not bothered by the cars, not bothered by the high heels and make-up. Each day tastes sweet. I feel in communion with the air of freedom.

A call from an anonymous number came to my cellphone as we were sitting in Stones. It was Nhlakanipho, asking for a cocaine dealer's contact. I sent him the number he requested.

"Hey, now I'm worried. Why does this cat want to buy cocaine this late at night? What if he wants to commit suicide?"

"He will never do it. He loves himself, he's a narcissistic character," Rasun said.

This did not allay my anxiety.

Nhlakanipho called again.

"Where are you guys?" Nhlakanipho asked.

I hesitated. "We are at Stones. We are about to leave now," I said, trying to discourage him from coming.

"OK, I'm already here in Obs," Nhlakanipho said.

I started shaking like a wet dog.

"What's the matter, are you sensing something?" Rasun asked.

"No, nothing," I replied.

Rasun was against the idea of Nhlakanipho joining us. He wanted to leave but I convinced him to stay.

When Nhlakanipho arrived, Rasun got up to hug him, as he had had a bit to drink. There was an air of mockery in the way they greeted each other. I was not happy to see Nhlakanipho. He did not waste any time in buying himself a beer.

We were sitting at our spot, the corner on the balcony. Nhlakanipho was trying to be civil with Rasun. They seemed to be getting along, or at least trying to. Nhlakanipho got up to go to the toilet.

"Your boy is on drugs . . . He's spending too much time in the toilet," Rasun said, after a few minutes had passed.

Nhlakanipho returned from the toilet sniffing. I too was convinced that he had been snorting cocaine. He faced us with the feigned confidence one gets from the drug. Rasun was telling us about his stay in Amsterdam. He went on about the different types of weed he sampled.

Rasun was a big fan of *The Godfather* movies. He and Nhlakanipho talked about the original film. I had never seen it.

"Yes, that Indian guy at the beginning says: 'I have raised my children in the American culture'," Nhlakanipho said.

Rasun's father is Indian and his mother is white. He is sensitive about race.

Nhlakanipho got up and went to the toilet again.

"Shit, I think there might still be a problem," Rasun said, his tone soft. "That comment about the Indian guy – Nhlakanipho was dissing me."

I shrugged.

"Come on, you're not stupid, don't tell me you didn't see that. It's a film about Italians; there are no Indians in it."

"Bra, I have never seen this movie before."

I sensed Nhlakanipho was standing behind the door listening to us.

"OK, I'll ask him when he comes back."

Nhlakanipho came from the left side. He had indeed been listening to us. He tried continuing the conversation.

"Bra, are there any Indians in *The Godfather*?" I broke in abruptly.

"Hee, Nhlakanipho, why are you bringing that up? I know you are not stupid," Rasun said, on his feet now. He held his beer tightly in his right hand. He looked like he wanted to pummel Nhlakanipho.

"Do you mean to tell me that guy is not Indian?" Nhlakanipho queried with exaggerated politeness.

"Come on, you fucking know he's not. It's an Italian movie."

"No, I don't know that."

"What are you on? You are a child," Rasun lambasted him.

Nhlakanipho put his hands together. It was getting stuffy for me. I left the guys and stood against the wall. I watched a couple playing snooker. I started getting cold from being on my own.

"We squashed the beef. I must be completely delusional," Rasun said as I came back to sit with them.

Nhlakanipho nodded. He started shaking with laughter, tapping Rasun on the shoulder.

Nhlakanipho waved a fifty-rand note in front of Rasun's face and asked him to buy another round of beers. From the way Rasun took the money and got up, I knew he was not coming back. Petty things like who sent who to buy smokes mattered to Nhlakanipho.

I was down to a couple of hundred rand in my bank account. I had paid the rent for the next two months from my salary, but after that I did not know what I was going to do. And it did not bother me that much.

Nhlakanipho asked about Rasun after an hour had elapsed.

"He probably left," I replied.

"What he did is not right," Nhlakanipho said with an exaggerated quaver in his voice. "He does not like seeing us together."

But Nhlakanipho knew what he had done to upset Rasun.

* * *

Nhlakanipho and I continued drinking at The Edge. He was now wrestling with quarts of beer. The tavern was packed with people, mostly students from CPUT. You could not turn around without bumping into someone. The room was filled with cigarette smoke.

Nhlakanipho returned from the toilet with white powder under his nose. He sat on a chair to my left. His eyes were bloodshot. He held a beer in his hand.

"That message you sent me . . ." he began, not looking at me. "Who will I call a friend, when I don't have you?"

This softened me.

"I understand . . . you are going through some changes. If you need space, it's fine," Nhlakanipho reasoned. "When I showed Mpumelelo that message, he thought we were fighting. I told him: you don't understand." He shook his head.

Nhlakanipho was attending a fashion show with his new girlfriend the following day. He had planned on snorting cocaine before going to the event. But he ended up using all the coke that night.

* * *

I tried waking Nhlakanipho in the cab. He had passed out on the back seat. I kept shaking him but he would not wake up. I would have to withdraw money. This was not part of the plan. Before we got into the cab Nhlakanipho had agreed to pay.

* * *

"You look upset," Nhlakanipho said.

The morning was dying. We had gotten out of the cab and drawn money at the Engen garage in Newlands, and Nhlakanipho was walking me home.

"How can I not be upset? I used the last of my money to pay for the cab. You have enough money for cocaine and beer," I fumed.

"Mangaliso, what is wrong with you? What are these funny messages you send me?"

"Dude, you don't have to walk me. Go home. Your place is in the other direction," I yelled.

I did not hear from him again.

* * *

Tongai woke me early one Sunday morning. It must have been five o'clock. He had clearly been drinking.

"Were you drinking with Nhlakanipho?" I asked.

Tongai nodded. "Nhlakanipho called me. I was in a public toilet. I said: 'Nhlakanipho, I love shitting in public toilets, I just love shitting in public toilets.'" Tongai shocked me.

"You almost ruined good friendships that were going to last a long time," Tongai said.

"Dude, I was trying to sleep."

"Oh, oh, I'm sorry," Tongai said, with his hands together.

Nhlakanipho would go on to pull the cab stunt on Tongai, too. He passed out and did not pay the cab driver. And so Nhlakanipho and Tongai fought. Tongai said he got the impression that Nhlakanipho and Mpumelelo were also vindictive towards each other.

* * *

Tongai entered the flat carrying grocery bags. He took a can of air freshener from one of the bags and sprayed around the lounge. We had never bought air freshener since we started sharing the apartment. Tongai's close friend Ntaba was coming to Cape Town, and we had agreed to accommodate him for a week. Ntaba's girlfriend was coming too, but she was going to stay at her parents' place in Muizenberg. Ntaba had graduated from UCT and gone on to work in Joburg. He was also Zimbabwean. On some occasions Ntaba had stayed with Tongai's mother when he was still a student. Tongai spoke highly of him and his girlfriend, who had been together since our varsity days. To Tongai, Ntaba's girlfriend was the sort of woman he, Tongai, would like to introduce to his grandmother. The couple had once visited Tongai's family in Zimbabwe. Tongai told me how good it looked: Ntaba and his girlfriend playing with the children.

A few days after arriving at our place, Ntaba bought some groceries and prepaid electricity. Tongai had borrowed a mattress from his mother for Ntaba to sleep on. He was jumpy around Ntaba. He even told Ntaba he was now sober. Ntaba seemed to be some authority in Tongai's life, folding his arms and nodding as they chatted.

* * *

One evening I found Tongai, his cousin Daniel and some other Zimbabwean guys in the lounge with Ntaba. These guys had never been to our place before. Ntaba had this gentle way of conducting them, and they laughed at the things he said. Ntaba was clean and laughed softly. The Zimbabwean squad then marched on to Rondebosch with Ntaba. I was not keen on going out.

In the mornings I would greet Ntaba and only see him again at night. He did not eat with us. His presence lifted Tongai. After Ntaba had returned to Joburg, Tongai told me about their outings to high-class spots in town. The girlfriend's family accompanied them one night. Tongai was impressed by how Ntaba would only have two drinks on a night out.

* * *

Some of the literature Tongai had been giving me included an essay by Thomas Wolfe titled "God's Lonely Man". He also suggested I read Sartre's *Nausea*. I read the essay; the heart of it was that loneliness was inevitable for the living. These ideas entered my chest and made sense to me. *Nausea* heightened this sense of nothingness. In the midst of these fumes of emptiness, I saw people on a train. There was a blind woman singing, accompanied by someone I thought to be her relative, who was shaking a silver tin. In their minds, people seemed to disappear. There was beauty in this, there was life in them. One woman was standing close to the door, her face coloured by freckles. I realised that existence is a wondrous taste. I got home and wrote a verse in my notebook. I called it "Unlike Nausea". Tongai would go on and say, "Hayi, you have made a one eighty-degree turn from *Nausea*."

I paused, but did not give more thought to his remark.

* * *

At about three in the afternoon one Sunday, I received a call from Paul inviting me to a braai at his place. He said he would meet me at the Caltex garage near my place. I left the flat wearing a navy jersey and black denim jeans. Paul smiled broadly when he saw me. The petrol cap of his blue Mercedes-Benz was open and an attendant was filling the tank.

Paul was my mother's friend. He had worked with my mother in Durban when I was twelve. Later, every Monday, he would send me a message inviting me to men's ministry. I never attended. I did not believe in God any more. Even at the braai, I was reluctant to hang with a bunch of Christians. They would probably set some time for fellowship. But the day had been grey and I wanted to get out of the apartment.

"How are things at work?" Paul asked.

We were driving up from Rondebosch to get onto the highway. Brown grass was waving along the side of the road.

"I resigned," I said.

"Oh, I'm sorry to hear that. You know, I could tell when you were coming up to me that you had been hurt."

This touched me – just to have someone who cared.

Paul put out his left hand and prayed: "I rebuke those demons that have been hurting Manga."

* * *

Paul was a black American who'd married a coloured woman from Cape Town. His wife was expecting their second child. They stayed at a villa in Century City. The complex looked expensive, the sort of places where rappers shot music videos.

I looked for Paul's features in his daughter and couldn't find them.

"See, this is not a chauvinistic house . . . I braai," Paul said with a fork in his hand.

160

The kitchen was decked out with all kinds of meat: burgers, boerewors, chicken. We all served ourselves. About eight brothers who attended Paul's fellowship were present.

Paul booked us movie tickets via the internet after we had all eaten. We drove to Canal Walk in two cars. At the cinema, I tried to make sense of the script. The film was a thriller with a comedic twist. The comic effort was not convincing. But because it starred two of Hollywood's shining faces it was bound to make money.

*　*　*

"McDonald's. There are too many of them," I said from the back of the car as Paul took me and another brother home.

He scoffed at my comment.

Before dropping me off, Paul muttered: "If you are going to read Malcolm X and about communism . . . The Bible says the curse of man is labour."

I found Tongai in the apartment. He had cooked supper. My stomach was still heavy from the feast at Paul's place.

"How can you have friends we don't know of, Manga?" Tongai cried out in the lounge.

The trip with Paul had lifted my spirits. And I explained this to Tongai.

"Paul is an old friend of my mother's," I said.

The late-night movie on TV was *Enemy of the State*, starring Will Smith.

"I don't like this movie," I said.

"Why not? It's one of my favourite Will Smith movies," Tongai said.

"I just don't like it."

"Have you seen *Terminator*?" Tongai asked.

I shook my head.

"I'm trying to figure out your favourite movies," Tongai said and put his hands together.

I stopped watching the film at the point where Will Smith was only using public phones to make calls, after discovering that everything else was bugged.

*   *   *

One Saturday morning I found a string of messages on my cellphone. Tongai was asking me to call him. *When someone does that, there's usually something wrong.* I had sent people messages when I was lying on the floor in Vredehoek. I went out, bought airtime and called him back. Tongai was locked inside Tagore's. He said he had passed out in the toilet.

I caught a taxi and got off in Observatory. I asked the manager of Revolution Records for the number of the owner of Tagore's.

"The owner is on his way," I said to Tongai, as I stood outside the front door.

A steel security door and a big padlock guarded Tagore's. It took no more than fifteen minutes for the owner to arrive. We had woken him from his sleep and he had not combed his hair. He seemed hung over.

I broke into laughter when I saw Tongai sitting inside. He had a beer in his hand and was going through some records in the rack.

Tongai walked out with the beer. I feared the owner would lambast him, but he said nothing.

"Oh, this is your friend . . . the one who was locked in," remarked the manager from Revolution Records as we were passing the store.

Tongai was keen on breakfast, so we went into Pancho's and ordered bacon and eggs. Observatory was quiet. There were a few people trickling in and out of the second-hand bookshop across the road. Tongai made fun of the incident at Tagore's, saying he was about to compose a jazz number before we walked in.

"Let's go to Trenchtown . . . Just for one drink," he suggested.

We had finished our breakfasts and were sitting at the table relaxing. For a while we argued about the merits of writing in one's indigenous tongue. Tongai said everything depended on money and that there had never been a Xhosa classic before. I said art comes from a different paradigm and that it becomes the property of a community, irrespective of commerce.

Surprisingly, Tongai had a lot of money to spend. When we got to Trenchtown, he knocked back three draughts in a short space of time. We sat close to a heater. Tongai said he was a disappointment to his grandmother. He did not speak to her; when she called, he refused to talk to her. His grandmother had warned Tongai not to be anything like his father. Tongai said his father was a terrible man.

"But you are not violent. You are calm, aside from the fact that you drink a lot and hurt yourself," I said.

"My father was also like that. He had a calm side but was also very violent . . . I was sitting at Mom's flat with my feet on the table trying to write in my notebook and Mom said: 'You are sitting judging the world . . . just like your father.' And since then I haven't been able to write," Tongai said.

Tongai's father had magical abilities. While his mother had a restraining order against him, he would show up in the elevator when there was no one around and say: "Did you think you could escape from me?" Tongai's mother also drank heavily. The times

163

I went to her apartment she would be drunk from finishing a few bottles of wine.

I told Tongai of my relationship with my father, and that the last time I saw him he wanted us to go for a paternity test. I had never told any of my friends about this. The last person I spoke to about my father was some guy I met at a bar. He just came in and sat next to me. This guy told me that he had stopped doing crime and was now trying to make things right with his daughter.

"I think each person has their journey and that's it," I said. "It becomes yours and no one else's. This world has this way of measuring people . . . but time also lapses and there's nothing you can do about it, I think the biggest lesson to be learnt is that of being a person . . . and that exists outside all these schools."

Kgotso and Michelle walked into Trenchtown holding hands. Kgotso was wearing a Kangol cap. He looked like a Sophiatown jazz cat. He suggested we join them at their table. They had all been drinking together the previous night at Tagore's. Kgotso laughed heartily when Tongai told them that he had spent the night there.

"Tongai, once you start you cannot stop, hey?" Kgotso observed.

Tongai had been drinking steadily since we got to Trenchtown. I had had a cup of coffee.

"I heard Ntaba was in town," Kgotso said.

Tongai nodded.

"How do you guys do it?" Kgotso asked. "Ntaba is a staunch supporter of ZANU-PF. His father is even a minister in the government."

Tongai put his hands together and smiled: "We agreed to disagree. We don't talk about politics . . . serious," Tongai said.

"That's very strange . . . That's like me chilling having drinks with a member of the IFP," I said, surprised.

Kgotso laughed at my statement. I didn't know that Ntaba's father was a minister in Mugabe's government. Nhlakanipho had once asked Tongai whether Ntaba really believed that the Zimbabwean elections were not rigged. Ntaba had been arguing that all was well with democracy in Zimbwabwe.

Michelle had a book of poetry on the table. I picked it up.

"It's by some writer who committed suicide," she said.

I flipped the pages, scheming through the titles.

"I once heard that the worst way of dying is drowning . . . because you go through all the emotions thinking you are going to make it, only to die," Tongai said.

Michele and Kgotso were living together in Observatory. They invited us to their place for Kgotso's birthday party, the following Saturday.

*   *   *

Humanity is cursed . . . There's a timeless witch doctor who walks across valleys . . . tirelessly. She cries for skeletons. She weeps for children being strangled. There are so many curses. These curses are constructed by men . . . Now they are killing foreign nationals. They have erected monuments to remember those who have fallen from these curses. But these monuments do not heal us. In the streets, women moan and climax pus. Sometimes a condom catches the yellow pus.

"Don't eat it . . ." I said to Tongai.

Tongai had whipped some eggs in a white bowl. He was about to fry them.

"We should fast today. This is a day for mourning," I said.

Tongai put the bowl with the eggs in the fridge and left for work.

I had woken up and written a poem I titled "A Curse, to Humanity". It was inspired by the xenophobic attacks that happened in 2008. I started crying. Then I saw a vision of a witch doctor walking. She too was crying. The pain from the senseless deaths squeezed my intestines.

All this death drags at my head. An avalanche of tears rises from my throat. The world is dying. It has always been about death. Everything on earth fades. And that is a perfection from God. Our bodies wrinkle over time. Nothing here is permanent. It is only God who does not wither. God endows us with gifts. For me, the word is my gift. It is a gift, that's why it overwhelms me. Sometimes I fear I won't be able to write another good passage because I don't know where it comes from. People lose it when they don't realise that their gifts are from God. That's when they self-destruct.

*   *   *

In my neglect I had forgotten smells. I lay on a bench in a park in lower Claremont and held an acorn to my nose. Mild grass covered the ground. There were also swings. The world has created its many chains: selling ideas to each other. The selling point for all these things is idolatry. Even for us who wanted to write, certain authors became our gods. The best book ever written is the Bible because the heart of it is peace. Some people can dwell on misfortunes and write about them. That only serves to kill. I have also been killing people with my pessimism. Today I am born a poet. It is only today that I start writing poetry. Tongai said his life coach was coming today. I want to share my words with them. The word is meant for communicating. And the best people to communicate with are those in the immediate surroundings.

Tongai got home at seven. He said he had broken the fast at his mother's place.

"Is your life coach not coming any more?" I asked.

Tongai shook his head. "You know, when you said 'let's fast', the first thing I thought of was . . . restoration," Tongai said.

In his room Tongai had a big sheet of paper with "fast for restoration" written on it. The paper had been on his wall for a couple of days.

I was haunted by a sense that something bad had happened. Earlier in the day I had called my grandmother, and she had said they were all fine at home. Still, my chest was buttoned with this restless feeling.

"Is your grandmother fine?" I asked Tongai.

"She's fine," Tongai replied.

"Do you speak to her now?"

"Ja," Tongai said.

"I can't help feeling that something bad has happened . . ."

Tongai sighed through his mouth. He sucked his tongue and swallowed.

"Six children . . . were killed in a taxi accident today."

"Where did this accident happen?" I asked.

Tongai did not reply.

"It's a terrible thing when children die," I said.

There was regret in Tongai's face.

* * *

One of my characters is from Khayelitsha. He is a student at UCT; he stays with his mother, who is a nurse, and his uncle. He will get excluded from UCT and get drawn into anti-eviction protests in Khayelitsha. Kwanele was involved in the anti-eviction campaigns, which occurred when people who could not pay rent were evicted from their homes in Mandela Park and moved to dog kennels in Site C. Huge chunks of land in Mandela Park are still owned by the World Bank. This was part of the package that came with the negotiations with the apartheid government. Kwanele, alongside fellow protesters, set light to government vehicles. The papers reported that this was thuggery posing as revolution. By going to a hip-hop gig in Khayelitsha with Moses, I hope to get a feel for the place.

* * *

I cannot seem to find Moses' shack. He says over the phone that I took the wrong taxi and that I should catch an iphela to Heideveld station. The sun is standing over Gugulethu. I am getting lost in the winding roads. A girl of about ten counts coins and gives me my change in a shelter where she sells airtime. Gugulethu is overwhelming me today. Sure, I have seen her stretch marks and wobbly thighs. I have even held her hand in public. I often thought she danced too much when she ought to be mourning. Who knows? Maybe Gugulethu needs to dance. And when the time is right, God will switch off the music.

The young girl's name is Sanele. It means "we are enough". Gugulethu will have to choose her messengers, not me. I cannot write for her. I know too little about her.

Moses stands in front of Heideveld station smoking a cigarette. He wears a friendly smile and beckons to me as I get out of the iphela. I shake my head when Moses tries to pass me the cigarette.

Inside the station, we run to an early evening train full of people. There are no seats available so we stand in the crowd in the carriage. A preacher works up a sweat. I laugh at him and also listen keenly. This too is a message. At some point I used to be impatient with preachers in trains. They have seen their truth.

The gig is in Litha Park. Moses leads the way as we walk along the tarred road. The streets are brightly lit. It is quiet; most people are in their homes.

"You have been quiet for a long time," Moses says.

"I needed to wash myself clean," I reply.

"Oh, you are a writer. That's what you are . . . a writer," Moses says.

The event is held at a sports ground with a pavilion. It is a free show. As we enter, some of the organisers ask for our details for future gigs and also hand us a newsletter. There are familiar faces in the stands. The spirit of the occasion is self-determination. Speakers call for hip-hop to set its own agenda outside of corporations. Some of them speak in American accents.

One emcee takes me with him as he raps. He speaks in his own language. He says his father used to come from work and go straight to the shebeen. He says he also could have been a gangster, and blamed everything on poverty. May God bless this phenomenal artist, open doors for him. The world needs such honesty.

It ends in violence. We hear reports of fighting outside the venue. Drunkards hijack the microphone. The host protests.

*   *   *

From the first clatter of dishes in the morning, I was up writing. My story was taking a surprising turn. Having written five chapters, it was high time I shared it with someone.

"Come, let me show you some of my work . . . I have been keeping it to myself for too long," I said to Tongai in his room.

"Aw, the poetry of Mangaliso Zolo," Tongai said scornfully. He then quickly put on an apologetic mask.

I started regretting the gesture. I went to the kitchen, leaving Tongai reading at my computer.

"Blaka blaka, Manga," I heard Tongai yell from my bedroom. "I like the voice."

"By that same token, can you lend me ten rand? I want to catch a taxi to Mom's place," Tongai said when I had returned to the room.

I was a little put off, though I still pulled out a ten-rand note from my wallet.

"And can you borrow me a bag?" Tongai asked.

I gave him a bag of mine.

"No, this one is too small," he said.

I pulled down a bigger bag from the top of my wardrobe.

"Is this one fine?" I asked.

Tongai nodded.

"What are you going to do with the bag?" I asked.

"Mom's," was all he said.

It was the Saturday of Kgotso's birthday. Tongai came back from his mother's place later in the afternoon. He was carrying a blue plastic bag.

"I bought some chicken," Tongai said.

"No, thanks, I'm fine."

I had just eaten an avocado. *Creativity is about life, the body has to be vital. The good ones create children, while the corrupted ones use sex for perversion. That's what the world does: pervert the good things of God. The oil from the chicken will suffocate the life in me.*

"Why don't you want my chicken?" Tongai asked, looking worried.

It is also essential that I humble myself to God. The chicken is also from God. I cannot deny myself the good things of God.

"No, it's fine," I said.

I got a knife and cut two pieces for myself.

"Are you not gonna eat?" I asked when I was done.

"No, no, I'm fine. I'm not hungry," Tongai said.

I wrote two chapters at supersonic speed. My head became a field with grassy ideas. There was something in everything.

*   *   *

"You know, I'm starting to agree with you about living in the now," Tongai said. "This thing of planning ahead . . . we might as well go to Kgotso's party carrying a coffin."

I laughed. We were walking to the Pick n Pay to get some snacks.

Later, as we were walking in Observatory on our way to the party, I saw some guys I used to stay with in res. We stood opposite the bottle store in Lower Main Road. There was a dark shebeen next to us. I had never been there in all my years of gallivanting in Observatory. It was sad to see my old friends. They were so far from me. Life had moved us apart. One guy even had a beer belly. I chatted with them in Sesotho.

"Hey . . . you also know language," Tongai sighed as we strolled to Kgotso's place, which was just down from Tagore's. There was a wooden carving that resembled a Red Indian pinned to the front door. The house was extensive, with a large yard.

Observatory is about images. My head is becoming light at these many appearances. The sky in these parts dances. The clouds are narrow. Me . . . I am water. I cannot be contained. On a silent bend, I sat on my own.

"Are you fine, Manga?" Kgotso asked.

"Sometimes I disappear into my head," I said.

"Sometimes it can be one voice," Tongai said, peeking from the braai stand. He was shaking. He had told everyone that he was not going to drink. I could tell that he was craving a drink.

"I'm celebrating. Caroline has agreed to go on a date with me," Tongai said later, taking gulps from a quart of beer.

Caroline was studying at UCT. I knew Tongai had a thing for white women. Of all the white girls he had approached, only Michelle had ever gone out with him.

A famous guitarist was billed to perform at Tagore's. We left the party, as people were starting to trickle off there. Tongai was elusive. He left and did not say where he was going. I sat on my own. A gentleman dressed all in black walked in. I recognised him; I had seen him playing in town before. He wore many earrings, some even in his nose. His ears were pointed like an elf, and his mouth was red from what looked like lipstick. *That's the thing with the arts; it becomes Satan's field.*

The star of the night played his guitar with lust. He shimmered in a white blazer. He looked otherworldly. I left the place with my throat dry.

I stopped a cab in Lower Main Road. The cab driver was calm and sat straight up in his seat.

"Do you go to church?" I asked while we were driving.

The cab driver nodded. "I play guitar in our worship team," he said.

"I've just come from a show . . . some guy was playing guitar. That's such a lustful instrument," I said.

The cab driver had a sleeveless jersey on. He was at ease. Somehow I just knew he went to church. He was not even fussy about how much I owed him. He was fine with the amount I suggested.

"So where do you go to church?" I asked.

"The Bible Tabernacle," he said.

"Man . . . I also want to go to church . . . I want to believe in God . . . I just need that gift of faith. How do I get to your church?"

"At the Mowbray taxi rank, there are buses designated the Bible Tabernacle. If you get there at seven in the morning, you can catch one of them. I hope to see you tomorrow. I believe God has a message for you," the cab driver said before dropping me off.

*   *   *

In the morning, I put back on the formal clothes I had avoided since I stopped working. I walked out of our block carrying my Bible. It was an uncertain morning; from the taxi, the streets were tiring. At the Mowbray taxi rank, I looked out for the buses the cab driver had mentioned. By eight I had not seen any of them. In front of the ticket boxes at the taxi rank, two witches were cursing. I asked them about the buses.

"Never . . . here, there are no buses," one of them screeched.

The cab driver's name was Paul. Perhaps the message was in the Bible. In my Bible, I could not find the book of Paul. It could be that I had bought a faulty Bible. A brother who walked past me was also carrying a Bible. I trotted up to him.

"Do you know where I can find the book of Paul?"

"There is no book of Paul. Paul only wrote letters."

"Where do you go to church?"

"My church . . . it's in Parow."

"Do you mind if I come with you?"

"No problem."

His name was Elio. He was from Mozambique. Before converting to Christianity, he had been a Muslim for ten years. He had also had a spell with drugs and alcohol.

"Oh, you can also sing," Elio said as we were waiting for the train at Mowbray station. I had been humming. "Our pastor teaches people the piano."

The people who sell train tickets were not on duty, so we just boarded the train. Along the railway line we could see cemeteries. I thought we were going to the land of the dead, only for us to surface again and pass some hills. Elio led the way out of Parow station. The tar seemed in motion from the glare of the sun. Parow was painfully quiet. Elio spoke in Portuguese to some brothers who were also on their way to church. *We can never fully comprehend God. His wonders can transpire in a foreign language. He will keep his secrets in the many languages.*

Because I was a first-time visitor to the church, I was asked to stand in the white hall with opaque windows. The pastor was dressed in white and he played the piano. He had a deep voice. I feared him. He seemed to be close to God. *When people are that close to God it becomes a calamity once they fall. The devil was also close to God. There is something devilish about the pastor. But his goodness I see in that he has children.*

A young preacher got up on the podium. Like me, he seemed uncertain of himself. He preached about the story of Jonah, his message being that God's plan is always greater than ours. There was a translator standing next to him. "You should stop listening to your own music and listen to the music of the Creator," he said.

I felt the sermon in my inner core. Elio called the pastor after the service. They spoke in Portuguese. Pastor Marquez smiled at me and asked me to accompany him to his office. I looked up to the windows at the top of the church. *This is the end. I won't be able to come out of here.* The pastor sat in a chair in the office and asked me my name. *He is going to read from the book of life.* I stammered and told him my name. Then I turned around and walked out of the office, breathing heavily. Elio was standing outside the door.

"What's wrong?" the pastor asked, coming out after me.

"Come on, go back inside," Elio said.

Now crying, I sat down again in the office.

"You know, I fear you . . . You seem to be so close to God," I said.

We knelt down and prayed. I accepted Jesus Christ and his purpose.

"You are now part of the family, we can even speak to your family for you," the pastor said.

I became nervous, remembering that Mfundo had said the same thing.

"You play the piano," I said to the pastor, as Elio and I were walking out.

The pastor smiled, standing in the doorway.

On our way back to the station, I sent Rasun a text message: "God is great." Rasun replied: "Dunsky, come back to me when you have found the secret number." I deleted his message after reading it. We walked down into the subway. One woman we passed had yellow eyes; I asked her if I could pray for her. In the shadow of the subway, I placed my right hand on her shoulder.

"That's amazing," Elio said after I had prayed for the woman.

Inside the train, my fingers felt sweaty. Elio was sitting next to me. The train rattled along the rails. We got off at Salt River.

"I know you, brother," a man said to me as we were walking out of the station. "Don't you remember me? I saved your life. I'm the security guard that called the ambulance for you in Vrede-hoek. I saved your life."

"Let's rephrase that; let's thank Jesus for using you to save my life," I said.

*   *   *

The television in the apartment was testing me. I fought back with the little knowledge I had of the Word. I uttered verses back at the screen. Tongai was also sitting in the lounge. Water was my salvation. When troubled, I would go to the sink and pour myself a glass of water. I begged Tongai that we not watch a programme on South African crime stories, as it was a condemnation to the conscience. Tongai was keen on finishing the programme. A man was said to have raped a four-year-old girl. He started to look like me.

All this condemnation is not right. I had also been condemning the world with my story. I got my flash disk from its hiding place at the top of my wardrobe.

"I'm deleting this story," I said, inserting the device in Tongai's computer.

"I urge you to think about this," Tongai cautioned.

"No, I have made up my mind," I said and deleted the work I had written.

If I am going into darkness, all I want to take with me are the Ten Commandments. Tongai and I scrambled through the Bible, looking for the relevant passage of Scripture. The Ten Commandments are all about not killing. There are many ways to kill: gossip is a form of killing; so is stealing.

I seem to have inherited Tongai's mental fear. My head was splitting into ideas in bed. I saw a vision of myself running in primary school. My life had always been a fight between good and evil. I had the lights on, though I was trying to sleep.

Tongai peeked in through the door: "You know, those kids who died in the car accident . . . one of them fell on the tar and split his head in two," he said.

PART 3
Before the Sun Rises

Evil need not come from one place. It can be a concerted effort from the disciples of witchcraft. I could not find my one pair of shoes in my wardrobe. My mother cried out: "It's Ma'Dlomo, she's taking the shoes to witch doctors." My grandmother confronted Ma'Dlomo about the shoes, and Ma'Dlomo said she knew nothing.

We prayed in the lounge preparing for my journey. My grandmother read a verse from the Bible. "It is this verse that makes me find myself going around the house three times, praying," she said. My mother had asked my grandmother to give a word. We were all holding hands in a circle.

As the bus was departing from King William's Town, my mother, grandmother and my aunt's daughter stood waving their hands. My grandmother looked mightily worried.

I sat in a window seat. I did not say anything to the person sitting next to me. I preferred not to eat solid food during the long journey; yoghurt was enough for me. The bus was getting stuffy as we reached Cape Town.

I wait for my luggage outside Texie's in Adderley Street. The morning sun is sharp on my forehead. As soon as one of the coach staff leaves the bus, people huddle around the trailer. He holds up my green bag and I walk over and show him my sticker. I drag my bag towards the station. A street kid runs up to me. I shake my head, refusing his offer to carry my bag. I know their tricks all too well: they will say they're not going to charge you, only to coerce you to pay them once they have carried your luggage.

The taxi conductor points me to the back seat when I tell him

I'm going to Kenilworth. My long bag is placed in the middle of the taxi. I hate sitting in the back seat. My knees are crammed, pressing against the seat in front of me. Driving through the southern suburbs, at a few minutes past ten, the streets are languorous. I have returned to Cape Town to clear the flat. I also hope to get my deposit from the agent. I should not spend more than a couple of weeks here. Tongai does not want to continue staying in the flat. I had suggested he take up the lease.

"I can't, man . . . it becomes impersonal, staying with a stranger," Tongai said.

Getting my bag up the stairs is hard work. I pull it up with my right hand, the wheels screeching and jumping on the stairs. It is lazily quiet in the flat. Tongai is still at work. I place my bag in my room. I still have a newsletter on global economics on the dressing table; I got this from the guys that had organised the hip-hop gig in Khayelitsha. I never got round to reading it. I glance at the title: "Global Economic Forum".

My toiletries are in a plastic bag. I take out my toothbrush and toothpaste and walk to the bathroom. There are two toothbrushes next to the bathroom mirror. This is strange, I think for a moment, brushing my teeth.

To pass the time, I decide to go to an internet café to check my e-mail. On Facebook I notice that Bridgette is online. "What's up?" I write in her chat box.

"Oh, you're back," Bridgette replies.

"How did you know I was gone?"

"Tongai told us."

This unsettles me. What exactly did Tongai tell them? And how did they contact each other? Bridgette was my pursuit.

*   *   *

Tongai comes home at his usual time in the early evening. He enters the flat sighing, saying he's tired. He kicks up his feet on the table and we watch TV. Tongai runs to the kitchen when a snake comes up on the screen.

"It's only on TV," I say.

"Still, I can't stand to see a snake," he says.

Tongai prepares to cook. He takes a pack of chicken breasts from the freezer and defrosts it with hot water in the sink. Tongai trots out the apartment to answer a call from his mother. "Moms," I hear him say on his way out. He returns and continues cooking. He chops two chicken breasts with a sharp knife on the kitchen table.

"So how's the book coming along?" he asks. He seems to have vinegar in his throat as he says this.

"It's fine," I say reluctantly.

At home, I had started on the book again. It was easy rewriting the chapters I had already done. I remembered most of the work that I had written. I am a careful writer. I go over my words many times. I only add new words after much consideration.

"Daniel was sleeping here while you were gone," Tongai says.

Tongai's cousin had had problems with accommodation before. He had stayed with us for two weeks then. The guys he was free-riding off had asked him to move out. What irked me about Daniel was his attitude that people owed him something. He became an inconvenience to us. I would have to wait for Daniel after work outside the flat. But this did not seem to bother him; he would stroll up to me rocking sunglasses.

"Oh . . . I was wondering why there were two toothbrushes in the bathroom."

"I hate this thing of his of calling in the dirt of midnight," Tongai says.

Tongai comes up to me to show the message he has received from Daniel. I do not look at the message.

"He's been sleeping here since Tuesday," Tongai says, on his way back to the kitchen. I have spent two weeks at home; it is Monday today.

Tongai pours a packet of pasta into a pot of boiling water.

"Bridgette and TK want to visit this weekend," Tongai says.

"Oh, I chatted with Bridgette on Facebook. How's she doing?" I ask, testing Tongai.

"I did not speak to her, I only spoke to TK," Tongai says.

I am tired from the long journey. I keep dozing off on the couch.

"I had such a good weekend," he says. "You know, I watched a very clever film . . ."

Tongai puts the pots on top of the side cupboard when the food is ready. We each dish for ourselves.

"Should I say grace?" I ask in the kitchen.

"No, I'll say it," Tongai says.

He finishes saying grace abruptly, almost as if something is moving in his chest. Tongai's standard of cooking has dropped since we started living together. His food just does not taste as good any more.

* * *

In the morning, on my way to the bathroom, Tongai asks: "Oh, is the music too loud?" He is ironing a pair of jeans in the lounge, wearing a shirt and boxers. The sound from his laptop speakers is not in any way loud. It could never be loud even if he wanted it to be.

"No, it's fine," I say.

I return to find Tongai holding a Bible. He is still in shirt and boxers.

"You know, the one thing I have realised is that there is nothing better than waking up and reading the Bible," he says.

I look at Tongai; his eyes fall to the ground. He dresses and leaves for work. It is a yellow morning. The sun streams through the window in my room. I make the bed, dropping all the linen to the floor and starting with the heavier items. While reaching beneath the bed, my fingers come up with a pink bra. Bridgette's name enters my head. I suspect Nhlakanipho has slept with her in my bed. This turns my head upside down.

"Dude, why is there a bra under my bed?" I ask Tongai over the phone. "What were you guys doing while I was gone?"

"I don't know . . . serious," Tongai says. "Wait . . . it could have been Daniel," he says after a while.

"So, he was sleeping in my bed?"

"Ja," Tongai says.

"No, I don't like what you did," I say, and drop the call.

Daniel works at the Cell C outlet in Cavendish Square. His phone goes straight to voice mail when I call. The one way for me to get the truth is to confront Daniel. So I exit the flat and walk to the mall. The employees at Cell C say they do not know where Daniel is. In a passage in the mall I see Daniel's tall frame. He is wearing the uniform black shirt and black trousers.

"Hey, Manga," Daniel says, smiling, as I walk up to him. "I heard what happened to you . . . some crazy stuff. But it happens."

"Did you sleep with a girl in my bed?" I ask.

Daniel takes a while to reply: "Ja," he says and nods.

"Thanks," I say and turn around.

"Hey, Manga, wait," Daniel calls out. "You seem upset."

"What you did is fucking disrespectful," I say.

"No, no, I did not sleep with her. We just played around a bit. She was having her period. Otherwise I would have slept with her."

"That is still disrespectful," I say.

* * *

If Daniel is covering for Tongai it would have to be a master plan. Since I'll be staying for only a couple of weeks, there's no point in me fighting them. I give Tongai the benefit of the doubt. I put my duvet and all my linen in the washing machine. The bra I put in a plastic bag and drop it in Tongai's room. To ease my suspicion, I call Bridgette.

"Did you sleep at my place?" I ask.

"No," Bridgette replies.

Bridgette is overtly sensual over the phone. She says she is looking forward to seeing me on the weekend.

Bridgette calls me back in the early evening. "Saturday it is," she says. I hear voices murmuring in the background. Her gesture turns me on.

"Ja," I say.

Not long after I have dropped the call, Tongai strides into the apartment. "Sorry about this weekend," he mutters. He is accompanied by Daniel and Nhlakanipho.

"We have brought this mfana to apologise," Tongai says, pointing at Daniel. Tongai makes his way to the kitchen. He pulls out a can of tuna from the cupboard.

"Like I said before . . . I'm sorry," Daniel says.

"Apology accepted and acknowledged," I say. "Though I will never know for certain what you guys were doing here while I was gone."

"Didn't you receive a phone call?" Tongai asks.

"What phone call?"

Nhlakanipho shakes his head in complete bewilderment at Tongai's foolishness.

"I thought the agent might have called you," Tongai quickly adds.

Tongai looks worried in the kitchen. "Nhlakanipho brought some of the clothes you left at his place," he says. Nhlakanipho passes a blue plastic bag of clothes to me. The T-shirt of mine that he was wearing the day Bridgette and TK visited is in the pile. He has a satisfied look on his face as I survey the clothes.

"So, how was home?" Nhlakanipho asks.

"It was great . . . it's always good to be with family."

"Did you see any regulars?"

"No, no one you would know. You don't know my friends . . . down there," I reply.

Nhlakanipho nods bitterly. "So, when are you leaving?" he asks.

"Sometime in the next two weeks."

"When exactly?" Nhlakanipho asks.

"Don't worry about that," I reply.

Tongai is out of sorts; he is panicking. He eats his sandwich standing up.

"So, when did you start sleeping here?" I ask Daniel.

"On Saturday," Daniel says.

"No, no . . ." Tongai says, shaking his head.

"On Wednesday."

"Oh . . . on Wednesday," I reply.

I had been watching TV before the guys came in. I have my pyjama trousers on. It is clear to me that Tongai is lying. But I won't confront him.

"That's a hot chick," Nhlakanipho says, looking at the screen.

"Yes, yes," Daniel says, nodding.

This is about all I can take. I excuse myself and go to my bedroom, but Nhlakanipho's high-pitched chatter disturbs my prayers. In time, the flat quietens down. Tongai has gone to see the guys out, I assume. Sleep does not come to me. I return to watching TV. On *Zone 14*, Maradona's uncle offers to sew a woman's dress. "You are a man of many talents, uncle," some girls comment. "Her life will end in tears," Maradona's uncle says, holding the dress. Prophecy comes in many guises. I was wondering why Nhlakanipho had a malicious look on his face when he gave me my clothes.

*   *   *

I set off at dawn to dump the clothes Nhlakanipho had given me in the rubbish bin. I don't know what else these guys could have doctored. I also get rid of the toiletries I left in the flat while I was away at home. Tongai did not sleep in his room last night. He must have stayed at Nhlakanipho's place. Even his laptop, which he usually keeps in the lounge, is not on the table.

Later in the afternoon, I read an e-mail Tongai has sent me: "I realise I'm the one that should be apologising, more than Daniel. I know this is not the first time I have betrayed your trust. I will be coming in late tonight as I'm working on my thesis." Tongai has attached to the e-mail a video of Alice Walker delivering the Steve Biko Memorial Lecture at UCT. He attended her talk with Michelle while I was at home. *What to make of Tongai's gesture? He's only apologising now that I have discovered that he was lying. I cannot go on staying with him. He is a dangerously manipulative character.*

So I call Tongai. "I read your e-mail," I say. "I'm not bitter at you,

I don't hold any grudges. But you have betrayed my trust and I cannot go on staying with you."

"Where am I going to stay, mfethu?" Tongai says, sounding sorry.

This shuts my stream of reasoning. *He is playing on my conscience.*

"No, I want you out. You can stay with your mother. I cannot trust you with the keys."

"OK," Tongai says softly.

"I want the keys back."

"I'll be at the African Studies library after work," Tongai says.

*   *   *

I haven't been to UCT since I failed my accounting exams. In the line waiting for the shuttle to Upper Campus, I spot a woman I once fancied. She gave me the run-around for a couple of years. She is dressed sportily, wearing black tracksuit pants. *She must be on her way to the gym.* "Hey, Naledi," I say, tapping her on her shoulder. She turns around and hugs me. But her distracted expression suggests she is not in the mood for chatting. Her head is elsewhere.

*   *   *

"I'm here on campus," I say to Tongai on the phone, standing on the steps in front of Jameson Hall. The UCT library is nearby.

"We have to meet after seven," Tongai whispers. "The library closes at seven."

I sit down on the steps and wait for Tongai. A statue of Cecil John Rhodes stands directly down from Jameson Hall. Someone once wrote some graffiti on the statue of the ancestor: "Fuck you and your ideas of empire."

A little after seven, Tongai approaches from the direction of the main library. He looks bulked-up, muscular. I had seen the trays of mass builders in his wardrobe. Something tells me that he is a soldier. It's in the way he walks. The arty front was never convincing.

"You can check them," Tongai says, taking the keys from a brown envelope.

I take a good look at the keys.

"When can I get my stuff from the apartment?" he asks.

"You can come in on Saturday."

"When on Saturday?"

"Any time."

"Morning or evening?" Tongai asks, with an undertone of anger.

I nod.

*   *   *

Naledi is walking along Main Road in Rondebosch. I jog up to her. "This is my exercise for the day," I say. Naledi smiles as she looks back at me. I really forced things with her. There were times she would not even answer my calls. But I would still persist. The last time I spoke to her, her father had passed on. Naledi is now doing her honours year. She has the neat beauty of a professional woman, with a thin mouth and a longish nose.

"I can't wait to get out of here," she says. "I'm so tired of this place. They want you to think in a certain way."

"You seemed to be cracking it. You were part of all those societies: investment society, Black Management Forum . . ." I remark.

At least Naledi is doing her honours in economics. It's a lot more interesting and meaningful than accounting. I wish I had majored in economics. Then I would have been doing something that engages my mind rather than just crunching numbers.

"Why the sudden discontent?" I ask.

"I'm just tired of this place. You know, earlier on in the year, I could not even get out of bed. I was depressed. I had to see a psychiatrist. It's only now that I'm getting out of it, though I still have my days."

"Maybe it's a late reaction to your father's passing," I say.

"That's what everyone is saying. The psychiatrist also thinks so. But I don't think it has anything to do with my father's death . . . You, how's the world of the working?" she asks.

"I resigned from my job. I don't even know what I'm gonna do next. I'm only here in Cape Town to sort things out with the flat."

"What happened?"

"I guess, like you, I also got tired of working a dead-end job. I needed to get out of there."

"You are supposed to be showing progress now," Naledi says.

"I want to give myself to God's seasons. Not measure myself according to the world: at a certain age, I'm supposed to be working a certain job and driving a certain kind of car. I have suffered from depression for what feels like forever. I think, now, I just want to do the things that I like."

"So what's your plan?" Naledi asks.

"I want to write; that's what I like doing."

"You want to write novels?"

"Poetry, short stories, whatever comes."

"I could always tell that there was something not quite right with you. Even on the day of your graduation," Naledi says.

"But I'm getting better now . . . I'm healing."

"No, you still look tired."

I shake Naledi's hand and leave her in front of her residence. A part of me wants to ask for her number, but I decide against it.

*   *   *

I think of Naledi while eating supper in the flat. Perhaps it's only now that I'm getting through to her. I had never imagined her as the type who would suffer from depression. She was always sassy and a fast mover, confident in her step.

At night, I struggle to sleep. From twelve onwards, I cannot sleep a wink. I try reading, but I cannot concentrate. The lights in my room are on until the sun comes up.

*   *   *

The agent says I cannot get my deposit back as I'm required to give two months' notice. The only hope I have of getting my money back is to find another tenant. Tongai offers to put an advert on Gumtree. In the advert, Tongai says the apartment comes furnished with a television. The TV is mine; Tongai even helped me carry it when I moved from Vredehoek. When I confront him, he says he forgot that the TV belonged to me.

Tongai contacts me after a couple of days, saying he's found someone who's interested in the flat. I agree to meet with the prospective tenant. On the day of our meeting, an hour goes by with no sign of him. *I'm starting to have my doubts about this arrangement.* He finally calls me: "Zolo . . . I'm sorry I'm late . . . I'm now on my way to Kenilworth." His thorny tone of voice scares me. *He did not sound like this the first time I spoke to him. And why is he now referring to me by my surname? This could be a witch doctor organised by Tongai's mother.*

"No, the place is no longer available," I say.

"No, no, no, Zolo," the guy cries out.

I drop the call. I cannot trust Tongai to find a tenant. This could give him leeway to bewitch me.

"Quit trying to find a tenant," I text Tongai.

"OK, the burden of finding a tenant then rests on you," he responds.

"Don't worry, you'll get your share of the deposit back," I reply.

I'm even willing to pay Tongai from my own pocket just to get him off my back.

Later in the day, Tongai sends me a message: "The groceries . . . can I also get my half on Saturday?" the message reads.

He is starting to get on my nerves. "You can take all the groceries," I reply.

I would rather sever all ties with Tongai now, give him his belongings and the groceries.

"Can you come get your stuff tonight?" I say to him over the phone.

"I can't . . . I'll be working in the library," he says.

"I'll pack them myself and take them to your mom's place."

"No, no, no," Tongai says, ending the call.

I need Tongai's mother's number, but his phone goes to voice mail when I call him. Daniel should have her number. In the afternoon breeze I hurry over to Cavendish Square. His colleagues at the Cell C shop again do not know where Daniel is. On my way out of the mall, I see Daniel sitting on a bench outside. He nods and looks the other way when I ask him for his aunt's number. He passes me his cellphone, which displays the number.

Tongai's mother does not pick up her phone. I leave her a message: "This is Mangaliso, the guy that stayed with Tongai; I need to talk to you."

I'm able to sleep from eight until midnight; then I wake up. I hear sounds of movement coming from the flat. It sounds like Tongai's door is opening and closing. But I'm too afraid to have a look. My eyes strain. I toss and turn until it is morning.

* * *

There are white plastic gloves next to Tongai's South African identity document. *What manner of being have I been staying with here?* Tongai is an agent for the Zimbabwean government. That explains his friendship with Ntaba. Tongai once told me that he knows of people planted at UCT to monitor Zimbabwean students. These people can take up to three years doing the same course, he said. Tongai has been killing people and now all the evidence is left with me. He does not really want to come and get his things. The night I was admitted to Groote Schuur, Tongai stepped on my foot at the Caltex store and apologised. Nhlakanipho turned around and did the same as Tongai. "I'm sorry," Nhlakanipho had said, with his hands together. I screamed and started breathing heavily. When I mentioned this incident to the doctor, Nhlakanipho denied it ever happened.

I do not want to start panicking. I step outside the apartment. The corridor is wet. Siviwe is in the parking lot holding a hosepipe, watering the flowers.

"You see, nothing came of the strikes," I say to Siviwe.

He nods thoughtfully. "But they could have stopped everything had they all joined the strike," Siviwe says. I leave him and walk up to my flat.

Murder is the case here. I'm developing a sense that someone has been killed. Maybe my grandmother was responsible for my grandfather's passing. My grandmother's last prayer at home was strange – her saying that she sometimes walks around the house three times. Those are things that witches do. The plastic gloves in Tongai's room could implicate me in the string of killings Tongai has committed. I have thrown those clothes of mine in the rubbish bin. This could be seen as attempting to destroy evidence. I need a witness, someone to show the things in Tongai's room. My head is becoming windy now. I descend the stairs to the ground floor.

The woman from the body corporate is kneeling in her flat as I stand outside the security door. There's something that looks like incense burning on top of a coffee table. She gets up abruptly on hearing my knock.

"There are some strange things in our flat. I'd like you to come up and see them," I say.

"You are the one who was holding a Bible and praying aloud . . . You upset a lot of the people downstairs," she says.

Who really are these people downstairs?

"I was admitted to a psychiatric hospital that night."

"There's no way I am going up there," the woman says and closes the door.

* * *

I'm alone in this. Tongai's mother is also part of the body corporate in her block of flats. These buildings are controlled by witches. The last time I saw Tongai's mother was at her place. Tongai just invited me to go with him to his mother's flat one morning. She was shaking as she opened the door. At the time I thought the shakes were from heavy drinking.

"I have cooked some food," Tongai's mother said.

We dished up some pork and potatoes in the kitchen. I noticed that Tongai was not eating but gave no more thought to it as the food was so tasty. Tongai returned his food to the pot. Maybe he had been trying to bewitch me with his cooking, and when he failed his mother decided to take matters into her own hands.

I'm afraid of taking my story to the police. They might think that I'm mentally unstable. I might even get locked up.

There is a friend of mine Tongai does not know, Nhlanhla. He is a Christian. We stayed together in the same residence in university. Nhlanhla was the first person to encounter my growing unbelief. I questioned him about Scripture, and he was unable to give me answers. The night I was at Groote Schuur, Tongai took my cellphone, which means my phone could be bugged now. So I call Nhlanhla from a public phone in Observatory. It's as if he was expecting my call. He quickly directs me to his place. Nhlanhla says he'll be waiting for me outside the house when I tell him I cannot use my phone.

There are drops of a tired sunlight in Observatory this Friday. I see faces I'm familiar with entering some of the pubs. I do not have the strength to greet them. The world is coming to an end. Two men are having simulated sex in a café as I walk past. The hands of the world are beginning to strangle the earth. "Greetings . . . shalom," reads a message from my home church. *Shalom* – where does this word come from? This is Freemasonry in operation. My mother could be involved with Freemasons.

* * *

Nhlanhla is standing in the street wearing a black hoodie. He lives in Little Mowbray, not far from the taxi rank, in a granny flat in his pastor's house. There's a green electric gate and a smaller gate at the front. There's also a block of flats in this street. Nhlanhla has recently graduated as an engineer and is still looking for a job. He leads me to the granny flat.

"My man, I was recently admitted to a psychiatric hospital," I explain. "I only spent one night there and was miraculously discharged the following day. Before that, there was so much that happened. I had even had a stint with drugs; I also resigned from my job. I did not want to blame anyone for my getting hospitalised. But going through some of the events, there was a strange lady that used to meet with my housemate in the flat. My housemate is Zimbabwean and yet he has a South African ID. I'm even scared of sleeping in that flat. I hear noises at night. I don't know. Can I stay here, just until I go back home? If you think there's something wrong with me, you can take me to a psychiatric hospital."

"I'll have to talk to my pastor," Nhlanhla says.

A few minutes later, Nhlanhla returns.

"It's fine, we can go get your stuff," he says.

This puts me at ease. We drive off in a monstrous vehicle to Kenilworth. No bullets could penetrate this car. This is all part of the plan. I had to be at Nhlanhla's place.

* * *

At the flat, I show Tongai's ID and the plastic gloves to Nhlanhla.

"Let's not jump to conclusions. Perhaps there's an explanation," he cautions. Then, looking at Tongai's identity photo, he says: "I know this guy."

This means the world to me. Tongai is identifiable to another person.

I quickly pack everything into my bag, including my notebooks and diaries.

"This is strange, that he would make you read this," Nhlanhla says, pointing at "God's Lonely Man". Tongai had suggested that I read the essay, saying it was an important bit of literature.

* * *

I sleep on a mattress on Nhlanhla's floor. In the middle of the night I awake and call out to him. "Sleep," Nhlanhla says. For the first time in a long while I'm able to sleep well.

* * *

A member of Nhlanhla's church has asked Nhlanhla to paint his bathroom ceiling. At eight on Saturday morning we are already in the flat in lower Kenilworth. The block of flats is near the station. The flat is compact, with a lounge and two bedrooms. The walls are painted white and the carpet is navy. As Nhlanhla scrubs the ceiling, I read my Bible in the lounge. The love of God brings tears to my eyes. What did I do to make God reach out? I do not have the answers. I was a sinful man leading a reckless life. It was mercy that saved me, more than love.

Tongai is coming at ten to get his stuff from my apartment, which is not far from here. Just before ten, I cross the railway line with Nhlanhla and walk to my block. We wait for Tongai inside. An hour goes by with no hint of Tongai. "On second thoughts, I'm coming at one," an SMS from him reads. This irritates me. I get the feeling that Tongai could be plotting with Nhlakanipho to drive me up the wall. We walk back to the flat we were painting.

Nhlanhla is calm as he continues painting the ceiling. "It will take several coats," he says, when I say I think the job is complete. Nhlanhla studied engineering; he is gifted with his hands. He is a man of order and structure – a builder. We make our way back to my apartment at close to one o'clock. Again, we wait in vain for

Tongai. We decide to leave after a while, as Nhlanhla tutors at Damelin on Saturday afternoons. In an act of wonder, the woman from the body corporate agrees to keep the keys for Tongai.

Nhlanhla has to do this job for the children; I cannot hold him back. He has to usher the new generation to a better place. We are pressed for time in the taxi. The taxi driver could not be bothered about us being late. Something is happening: the streets are spinning; time is coming to an end. Nhlanhla gets off in Rondebosch. He leaves me with the keys to his granny flat. My journey extends without him to Little Mowbray. A child standing in a garden in Nhlanhla's street scratches his head wildly. *There is a plague in operation.* I am pleased to have made it to Nhlanhla's house; I thought I would get lost.

I lie on the shadow of Nhlanhla's bed, restless, my chest heaving. Nhlanhla's pastor calls me outside. *They are building a new world here.* The pastor has bought the house recently. I help carry in some of the trees they are planting. This is one of the compounds that won't be harmed in the imminent destruction. But, in this new world, it's still a black man that does the gardening. That's the part I haven't figured out.

Nhlanhla returns in the late afternoon. I am relieved to see him. His presence calms me.

"I still have that song you guys recorded," Nhlanhla says, facing his computer.

"We were young . . . we did not know what we were doing," I say. "I no longer want anything to do with hip-hop. It's too aggressive."

Nhlanhla plays some of his Christian rap, much to my consternation. It's not so much what they are saying, but rather the spirit of the beat. Demons could dance to it.

"Could you please play something else, some good old singing?" I ask.

Nhlanhla only lowers the volume of the music. There is one song that I like. It speaks of Paul being a persecutor of Christians. So Paul is also not blameless.

In the breath of evening, Nhlanhla leaves for a dinner for couples organised by his pastor. In heaven, lovers will enter in pairs.

I have found the real Paul in Nhlanhla's pastor. He looks majestic. This is the Paul from the Bible. "They just want to smell you," Paul says as two dogs come up to me in the main house. Usually I would have been scared of the dogs, but I'm in such an uncertain place that they do not bother me. This is all part of the plan: Paul is keeping animals for the new world.

"Were you watching movies on Nhlanhla's computer?" Paul asks.

"No," I reply, shaking my head.

Paul hands me a book from his bookshelf. He is preparing a sermon for tomorrow. The world will be held and Paul will give a summary of life and lead us into the new time. I become drowsy reading the book in the lounge. But this is a test; I have to complete the book. The work is a manuscript . . . it is never in vain; even the works we do not finish are recorded.

"Do you eat pork, Mangaliso?" Paul asks from the kitchen.

Jesus cast demons onto the swine. But the pigs are also God's creation.

"Yes," I reply.

Paul is my ultimate judge. He too is a writer. Once he has assessed me, he will decide whether I am fit to join the chamber of writers in this house. In these walls I will be preserved like a mummy. I am already dead.

We eat in the kitchen, sitting at a round table; to my right are white cupboards. Paul's wife is also present. I do not have any appetite for the food. They are taking me back to the beginning of time with the ribs. Eve came out of Adam's rib. I explain to Paul the events that happened before my breakdown and of the witch doctor that used to come to the apartment. I realise as I am talking that I have food in my mouth. I pause to chew properly. Paul and his wife look on intently. Paul's wife has the face of an angel. She has heavenly blonde hair. I leave my plate half-empty.

I continue reading in the lounge. I struggle to concentrate. My eyelids are closing, but I'm afraid to sleep. Blood pounds in the veins in my mouth.

* * *

As I'm about to fall asleep, Nhlanhla wakes me. I'm grateful he has saved me from dying. We have to finish painting the ceiling in Kenilworth. We drive to my old neighbourhood in a minibus. The night is whispering about the streets. I'm hearing voices in the back seat. They are confusing me. I follow Nhlanhla as he climbs the stairs to the flat.

I sing as Nhlanhla layers the paint on the white ceiling. This is the only contribution I can make to ease the burden for Nhlanhla. In a better time, people will give whatever gifts they have willingly. "And so they grew in numbers," echoes in my head. It is a verse from the Acts of the Apostles.

The bathroom is filled with paint fumes. Nhlanhla encourages me to rest in the lounge. I do not want to seem lazy. I'm still coming to terms with what another Paul has said to me, that the curse of man is labour. I had just resigned from my job and was telling Paul that.

"Go take a break, you can come back," Nhlanhla says. I step on the black refuse bags on my way out.

My mind is the enemy. I cannot rest. Not when there's so much wind in my chest and in my head. The Bible is indicting me. I rise to my feet in such moments and look out the window. My ears are a chimney. I pray for calmness.

Nhlanhla and I have been called for a cause. It won't be easy. I run to Nhlanhla in the bathroom and read him some passages of Scripture. He listens and encourages me to be calm.

In the night, Nhlanhla prepares a bed for me in the owner's room. I try forcing sleep, closing my eyelids as my heart jerks violently. *When the Son of Man arrives, he will even utilise technology. Below the window in this room, a helicopter will wait to take us to heaven.*

* * *

Nhlanhla washes his hands in the basin in the morning. "You kept me up all night," he says. I remembered running to Nhlanhla after I thought I had heard the trumpet's call. I was not able to sleep at all. It is done. Nhlanhla clears the newspapers and the refuse bags from the bathroom. I help him carry the washing machine back to the bathroom.

"Now is the time to stop doubting and just believe," I chant outside the bathroom.

I am using the mantra I learnt at the Hare Krishna temple. I never did understand the meaning of the mantra. "That does not matter; the effect of the mantra is still achieved, even if you don't understand it," a temple elder advised.

My heart is wheezing as we walk in the corridor. Outside, I see the old woman, who was barking at Groote Schuur the night I was admitted, walking in the direction of the train station. She is still wearing blue hospital robes. I struggle up the hill to Nhlanhla's church in Mowbray. "I am running out of breath," I say to Nhlanhla. I hope to take a breather on a swing in the park.

"We are almost there," he says.

The kingdom of heaven is at stake. I force myself to continue.

*　*　*

The Message church looks different from the last time I attended. I don't know whether they have changed the venue. I pick up one woman's water bottle and drink from it as the congregation worships. The woman looks at me and smiles. *This is the kingdom of heaven: no one owns anything.* The water does not quench my thirst, though. My throat has become acidic.

From the pulpit, Paul gives his summary of life. I do not follow his words. I fidget in my seat. I feel we are entering heaven. But judgement still has to take place. Another preacher takes over after Paul. This will be an endless sermon. We will wait for Christ through preaching.

Perhaps heaven is like a game we used to play at crèche: we'd sit in a circle and the teacher would ask us to get up from our chairs; we'd have to run back to our seats and the teacher would have removed one chair; whoever was not able to find a seat would be out of the game.

Tea and cake is served after the service. Everyone in the church has a name tag except for me and Nhlanhla. I feel like an outsider in this heaven. Speaking to the other church members gives me the chills. I try to make conversation but my skin becomes watery. And whomever I talk to seems like a demonic creature.

"They're here," I say to Paul at the back of the church, panicky.

Paul pauses: "My wife is an occupational therapist," he says. "We have given your situation some thought. We don't think it's spiritual. Are you on medical aid?"

I shake my head.

* * *

The lanes read: Trauma and Emergency. It is hot in the car as we drive to Groote Schuur. This time around I do not have any fight in me. I am like any other mental patient. I do as I am told. I give them my arm when they want to check my blood pressure. It is a tiringly painful Sunday. The doctor on duty is a dark-skinned man. He pricks my finger for his tests. Nhlanhla leaves with Paul. They leave me in an empty room.

I find myself behind white bars. There is one security guard sitting behind a desk. He operates the gates to this section. There is lighting in this cold space. I sit on a plastic chair. Next to me are two women wearing blue hospital robes. We are all waiting for our turn to see the psychiatrist.

The psychiatrist is Indian. I sense that he's Muslim. His questions terrify me.

"May I pray?" I ask the psychiatrist.

"Sure, you can go ahead," he says.

I cannot pray. I am facing the devil. And the worst part is that I cannot get out of here. I start pacing around the room.

"It looks like you are regressing," the psychiatrist says. "We have to take you back."

They are taking me back to the living. A security guard walks me to a ward full of sick people. There are three nurses working here. They advise me to sleep in my allocated bed. I see a line of people walking up the corridor. This is judgement. The man next to me wakes up. The dead are rising. My presence is needed here to help the dead to rise.

One patient is carried out in a black bag. The confirmation of my death will be me seeing myself standing, wearing a black suit. That's when the matter will be resolved. I am starting to itch. I scratch my arms and my back. My whole body is itching. I stand on the floor. With my right hand I hold on to my head. The psychiatrist observes from a chair in the corner, writing in a folder.

Deep into the miserable night a lady nurse asks me to follow her. I shiver in the corridor, waiting. As I'm about to fall asleep on a chair, she wakes me.

"God will never shame us," I say to her.

"Oh yes!" the nurse shouts.

* * *

I have been called here to save the lost. The patients in the ward are watching TV.

"Switch this thing off. You are destroying these children," I say and switch the TV off.

"Hey, hold on," the security guard says and switches the TV back on.

* * *

The nurses serve us breakfast in the morning. I say grace before eating. I sit in a chair facing the window. There's another patient to my left. We are both wearing blue robes. When the other patient is finished eating, he licks his plate like a cat.

"He has a big appetite, from tik," one of the nurses says. A nurse observes us as we take our medication. The other patient returns to his bed. He seems to be able to sleep. I can't.

I am freezing. The one blanket is not enough. I see lines of people entering the hospital while looking out the window opposite my bed. They are being called to judgement. The hospital is a safe place for me to be. There's a patient who is kept in solitary confinement. The security guards take him out. He runs and tries to dive through the window glass. He stands up, shaking his head.

The TV has been playing the same episode of *Generations*. It ends in the same sad laugh. In total, there are three of us patients. The one resembling a cat is sitting on the middle chair watching TV. Now is the time for every knee to bow. I kneel in front of him.

"Hey, hey, get up," the security guard says, pulling me up.

* * *

Tongai predicted my end: "You will die a social death," he announced one afternoon after work. I looked at Tongai; he put his hands together and looked the other way. I laughed quietly, not knowing what to make of his statement. My books are all that connect me to the other world. They are safe with Nhlanhla. He can keep them and tell people who I was.

* * *

Ndlela's father is the only black man who has ever shown me love. He came to my award ceremony in high school. After I had come down from the stage, he shook my hand. Remembering this makes me cry. I sob in the bed.

"You have never been loved," Nhlakanipho once said. Perhaps he was right. I have never understood love. And hence I did not know God. The ultimate love was being crucified for the sins of the world. Love is taking the blame when you are not even sure that you were at fault. These things make me cry.

I remember beautiful artists. They have a gift of seeing beyond conditions, and draw us to the blackness of uncertainty. That's what art should achieve: point out the other side. Art is not there to unearth any truths, but rather to show the multiplicity of the nature of things. Young emcees stand on stages and prophesy, though only a few people listen to them.

It would seem we are in a season of mourning. Singers are crying on CD covers. The professional mourner is the artist. He cries for a living. He cries in order to live. They sing many songs bemoaning the loss of our cattle. The cattle will come back in a different way. It will take a spiritual awakening.

*   *   *

The security guard who works at night has a hoarse voice and is light-skinned. I suspect he smokes, from the sound of his watery throat. My grandfather was also light-skinned and a heavy smoker. I follow the security guard as he leads me to the shower. I pass him my robes over the top of the shower door. He waits for me outside. The water is lukewarm; I only have soap to wash with.

*   *   *

I cannot sleep at night. I am starting to feel claustrophobic. I want to get out of here.

"Please let me go . . . I want to be with my family and friends," I cry out to the nurses.

"Go back to your bed and sleep," the security guard advises.

I do as he tells me.

I do not know what the time is. Nor do I know the day of the week. All I know is that it is another morning. The madness is in the food. It is the food that keeps me in this place. I say grace before eating. I do not speak to the other patient. With his slimy black hair, he looks like a cat. I swallow my pills with some water and return to lying in bed.

"Come, Zolo," a nurse calls me out from the blankets.

She decks dominoes on the table and explains the rules of the game to me. Other nurses play with us. In a strange string of good fortune, I win all the games.

"You have won, Zolo," the nurse keeps on announcing. Then one of the other nurses wins a game. "He has won now," the nurse says.

"Congratulations," I say, and shake the victor's hand.

"He congratulated him," one nurse cheers.

* * *

Kwanele told me that they evaluate you through such games. I return to brooding on my bed. I do not have the stomach to watch the TV. I am in a mental institution. Here they institutionalise one's mental condition. The world has been in the business of assigning names to things. Even AIDS is just a name. But once you hear that diagnosis, it traps you.

* * *

I have been seeing the doctor walking in the corridors. I have not spoken to him since being admitted. The doctor has a crooked walk; he is wearing a yellow shirt.

"Please follow me to my office," he says, standing in front of me.

The office is nothing but a small room with a bed and two chairs.

"Religion means a lot to you," he says, holding his file.

"I'd rather not talk about issues of faith," I say.

I believe the doctor is Muslim. And so I want to avoid conflict. He does not recognise Jesus as the Lord and Saviour.

The doctor is asking me how I have kept alive since my resignation. He is questioning my very existence. My head is thin; I do not have the capacity to answer his questions. We are going around in circles.

"What happened the last time you were admitted here?" the doctor asks.

"I woke up to find my mother praying at the bedside. She cut my toenails and I was discharged."

* * *

I scream at night: "Please let me go; I want to be with my family." I force myself to the nurses' room. There are female patients in another room. They have long wild hair. The security guard comes after me; he asks me to return to bed. I feel comfortable with him. This is my grandfather; he has come from the dead to protect me.

My grandfather was a man of music. He was a choirmaster. Music is the ultimate godly gift. It is a higher state of communication. My grandfather is calm and assured of his musical abilities.

"Come wash, mfethu," my grandfather says.

"All right, father," I say and follow him to the showers.

I am uncertain with my feet on the tiles. Is this all a test? Will I even be able to come out of the shower? Luckily, when I'm finished washing I call out and grandfather gives me new robes.

* * *

I have resorted to washing off the pain with song. I sing songs about love. These bring tears to my eyes. Song is the answer to my problems. I vibrate my vocal cords and sing for mankind: "Bawo Thixo somandla kuyintoni na? / Emhlabeni sibuthwel ubunzima" (God Almighty, what have we done? / On earth we carry burdens).

I pray for curses on children to be removed. All this makes my throat lumpy. I never stop shivering. The cold in here never ceases and they refuse to allow me to bask in the sun.

"You have a visitor," says the security guard that works during the day.

My mother is in the reception area wearing a sporty jacket. She embraces me as if she can charge me with her heart. She looks lost and worried.

"Have you spoken to Doctor Lagada?" she asks.

"Yes, I have, a few times."

My mother's banter keeps me going. She fills the cold void of silence. She is resilient. She hasn't given up.

"Don't you want anything from town?" she asks.

I didn't celebrate my birthday this year. I didn't even tell anyone at the office that it was my birthday. I need to learn to love myself first before I can love others.

"I'd like some cake," I say.

My mother comes back in an hour carrying a square white box. I nibble on the cream from the cake while sitting on the bed. For a while, I bury myself in the delicacy. It leaves mounds of soil in my throat.

The hospital workers are endlessly on the move. They pass me, shuffling their shoes quickly. New people come in the evening.

* * *

Something strange happens in the night. I look up to find a male nurse sitting at my feet. He has a bag slung over his shoulder like Mfundo. He gets up and walks away when he realises that I'm aware of his presence. His gait is exactly like Mfundo's, but the only difference is that he appears to be coloured.

Under the glare of the lighting, I ponder this incident. I do not have the strength to question things extensively. I let it slide. They have taken the feline patient to Valkenberg. His mother came to give him more clothes. She was wearing a black veil that covered her head and neck.

They also want to take me to Valkenberg. "We received complaints about him last night, again," Dr Lagada says in his office.

My mother pleads with the doctor: "Could you please refer him to a hospital closer to home," she begs.

"We will admit him as an involuntary patient," Dr Lagada affirms, when my mother refuses to sign the papers for my admission to Valkenberg.

"Please, Dr Lagada," my mother begs, sounding desperate.

If this is your will, God, then let it be. I'm more worried about my mother than about being institutionalised. I wonder how they will take me to Valkenberg. I'll probably be transported in an ambulance escorted by security guards. I'm familiar with Valkenberg from visiting Kwanele there a few times. I know you start off in a ward with new patients. Once you improve, you graduate to spaces that are less confined. They even allow you to take walks around the hospital when you are almost ready to be discharged. So this is what they did to Kwanele; they gave a name to his illness and trapped him in the name of that illness.

Dr Lagada calls me to his office in the afternoon. The male nurse who looks like Mfundo and carries a bag is also in the room.

"So, how are you feeling now?" the doctor asks.

"I'm feeling better."

"Were you able to sleep last night?"

"I rested," I say after some thought. But I did not sleep a wink.

"You are looking a bit better. How's the anxiety?"

209

"It has ceased; Jesus healed me," I say.

"How?" Mfundo's lookalike howls.

"He died for my sins on the cross," I reply.

"How?" Mfundo's lookalike asks again.

This is all that I can take. I turn around and walk away.

"You see, he's passive-aggressive," the male nurse shouts as I walk out.

* * *

So this is how it comes to an end. My mother works around the clock calling people, asking for help. I become aware of lapses in time through my mother changing outfits. She hasn't stopped praying. We close our eyes and ask God for assistance in the reception area. I have made peace with my fate. I'm more worried about how the people at home will take my hospitalisation. It will certainly upset my grandmother a great deal.

"Grootman, you must pray that you never suffer from mental illness," I say to the security guard. "They are taking me to Valkenberg."

"In my whole time here, I haven't seen anything wrong with you," the security guard says.

"They say I behave badly at night," I say, and start crying.

I take my tears to my bed. My time is dying as I sit on the white sheet. Security guards and nurses pass me. Dr Lagada looks distressed doing his rounds in the hospital. In the evening the nurses add new medication to my usual dosage. For the first time I'm able to sleep at night. I wake in the morning with my head clearer.

The ward manager questions me after breakfast. He has a white scar running down the right side of his face. He stands next to my bed.

"I'm fine . . . just agitated, I want to be home with my friends and family," I say.

He asks me roughly the same questions as the psychiatrist who attended to me the night I was first admitted to Groote Schuur. He even uses the trick of asking, "You are from East London, right?"

"No, I'm from King William's Town," I reply.

The ward manager writes everything I say in his file. He leaves after the brief interrogation. He gives me hope: something good can still happen.

In a matter of about thirty minutes, we learn that the ward manager has approved my mother's request that I be moved to a hospital closer to home. I cannot contain my excitement as we wait for Dr Lagada's letter of referral. Dr Lagada gives my mother the letter and wishes us luck. "Thank you," I say to the doctor. I say goodbye to the security guard as he opens the gate for my final departure.

Kwanele once told me that a man walks tall when coming out of a mental institution. It is a new day; on the streets they are stringing up newspaper headlines on lamp posts. "I don't understand why Dr Lagada had to lie, saying he had received complaints about your behaviour last night," Mother says. "The ward manager said that they did not receive any complaints about your behaviour last night."

We wait for a taxi in a bus shelter. A cold wind is blowing. "There was also a strange nurse . . ." my mother says. "That one who looked like a moffie, who was carrying a bag the whole time. Can you believe he said to me: 'I know you. You came all the way from East London.'"

* * *

Tongai did indeed take all the groceries. He has cleaned out all the food from the cupboard and the fridge. All that remains of Tongai are four of his boxers hanging in the shower. My mother advises me not to sleep in my bedroom. "I have also been sleeping in the lounge," she says. "There's a lot of shuffling that happens in this block of flats, especially when it hits midnight."

* * *

In the late morning, we leave the apartment keys with the lady from the body corporate for collection by the agent and catch a cab to the airport. The cab drives slowly up Liesbeek Parkway. We pass shantytowns on the sides of the N2.

SONGEZIWE MAHLANGU was born in Alice in 1985. He matriculated from Dale College, in King William's Town, and now lives in East London.